Under

the

Light

Under
the
Light

A NOVEL

by Laura Whitcomb

Houghton Mifflin Harcourt
Boston   New York   2013

Houghton Mifflin is an imprint of Houghton Mifflin Harcourt Publishing Company.

www.hmhbooks.com

The text of this book is set in Walbaum.

Poem on p. ix reprinted by the permission of the publishers and the Trustees of Amherst College from THE POEMS OF EMILY DICKINSON, Thomas H. Johnson, ed., Cambridge, Mass.: The Belknap Press of Harvard University Press, Copyright © 1951, 1955, 1979, 1983 by the President and Fellows of Harvard College.

Library of Congress Cataloging-in-Publication Data
Whitcomb, Laura.
Under the light: a novel / by Laura Whitcomb.
pages cm
Companion book to: A certain slant of light.
Summary: "Helen needed a body to be with her beloved and Jenny needed to escape from hers before her spirit was broken. It was wicked, borrowing it, but love drives even the gentlest soul to desperate acts." — Provided by publisher.
ISBN 978-0-547-36754-5
[1. Ghosts — Fiction. 2. Spirit possession — Fiction. 3. Love — Fiction.] I. Title.
PZ7.W5785UN 2013
[Fic] — dc23
2012033303

Manufactured in the U.S.A.

DOC 10 9 8 7 6 5 4 3 2 1

4500406804

Acknowledgments

Thanks to my family, especially Cyn for Binny-sitting
and Binny for being such a good sport; my essential and
overlapping circles of friends (WSG, Chez, SRS, Revels, and my
supernatural tea partyers); my fabulous agent, Ann Rittenberg;
and my awesome partner in lit, editor Kate O'Sullivan.

For my son, Robinson David, my Binny. My spirit is made young, my heart full, my world new.
Oh, the cleverness of you.

Under
the
Light

Under the Light, yet under,
Under the Grass and the Dirt,
Under the Beetle's Cellar
Under the Clover's Root,
Further than Arm could stretch
Were it Giant long,
Further than Sunshine could
Were the Day Year long,
Over the Light, yet over,
Over the Arc of the Bird —
Over the Comet's chimney —
Over the Cubit's Head,
Further than Guess can gallop
Further than Riddle ride —
Oh for a Disc to the Distance
Between Ourselves and the Dead!

Emily Dickinson

PART 1

CHAPTER 1

Jenny

I USED TO PRACTICE LEAVING MY BODY. Closing my eyes in the shower, letting the spray beat on my forehead, forcing my pulse to drop. I'd breathe in the steam as slowly as possible. I'd pretend to drift out of my flesh and over the top of the shower curtain, slip out the open window.

The first day that it actually worked, it lasted only a few seconds. I was in bed, in the dark, too restless to sleep. I imagined I was a shooting star falling backwards away from earth, and the next moment I wasn't under the covers anymore. I opened my eyes to find myself cocooned between silver foil and cotton-candy-pink insulation, planted halfway in my bedroom wall. I could lean down and look out through the wallpaper. At first it felt normal. My body lay below like a crash dummy, pale and too stupid to save itself. *Is that what a dead body looks like?* Then the idea of being dead made my spirit zip into my flesh again so fast, the mattress shook.

But the second time, when it really worked, I wasn't thinking about leaving my body at all. I didn't even realize what was happening until it was too late. Some part of me decided to escape without needing permission from my brain.

∽

For the first fifteen years of my life, I had survived lots of bad days and never once ran away from home. Like the afternoon my parents discovered the photos I'd taken of myself — I never saw that camera again. I should have stashed the pictures in a better place. I thought I'd been more clever about hiding my diary. Still, on the day I left my body, I came home from school and found my father was holding it in his hands.

For such a small book it held an enormous weight — the most disturbing things my father could imagine, I guess: my true thoughts and feelings, things about me he had no control over.

My parents had been giving me a hard time that week because I didn't get straight-As on my midterms. They couldn't understand that I wasn't slacking off — I was sick. I couldn't sleep for more than ten minutes at a time. Light bothered my eyes. Sudden sounds made me jump and want to cry.

According to my father, the problem was that I was failing to live up to my potential. He reminded me that the devil tempts us with idle distractions.

I was in trouble so often, I'd gotten in the habit of pretending not to understand that my faults were sins, then acting grateful when my parents taught me the right way to behave. That worked for the little stuff: failing to excuse myself from a sex education lecture at school, talking to a strange man in the grocery store parking lot who wanted directions, walking to the park without asking permission. But this was serious, worse than the photos of myself that my father fed into the shredder.

Now, with my secret writing in his hands, my father looked victorious. *I knew you were wicked,* his eyes told me. *And you've proven me right with your own words.*

The Prayer Corner, at one end of our family room, was just three chairs used for family Bible study, prayer, and punishment. My mother and I sat down in our usual seats, but my father wouldn't sit.

"Is this a true reflection of your soul?" he asked me.

Why hadn't I kept it in my school locker?

"You may answer," he said, as if I was waiting for permission to speak.

"I don't know." In my mind I ran through what I'd recorded on those pages. *What was the worst thing?*

"Your mother and I live our lives before you as daily examples of walking with Christ," he said, "but it seems we've been giving you too many freedoms."

He set the diary on his chair and slipped a shiny black square from his pocket. As he unfolded it, I saw that it was an extra-large garbage bag. I felt like a kitten about to be sacked and drowned.

He didn't command us to come, but when he walked out into the hall, my mother followed, so I did too. She glanced back at me, and I thought her face would be stiff and angry, but she looked afraid. Maybe I wasn't the only one who had a secret diary tucked away.

When we got to my bedroom, my father was already sliding around hangers in the closet, examining my clothes. He studied my skirts and sweaters, dresses front and back, leaving some items on their padded hangers and slipping others off, letting those drop into the sucking black hole of the garbage bag.

I knew why he took away my blue tank top and the cotton

camisole; the necks were a little low, the straps narrow. But I could only imagine why other items were unacceptable. My black jersey jacket. Was the cut too rock-and-roll for him? And my brown knit skirt. It was expensive, from Nordstroms, one my mother picked out. She gasped as he unclipped it from the hanger, but when my father paused, not even looking at her, she put a finger to her lips and said nothing. Was it because that skirt came more than an inch above my knees?

He opened my dresser drawers and began to rifle through my underwear. I felt dizzy. Not because my father was touching my panties and bras, but because I was afraid that when he got to the lowest drawer he'd discover the false bottom and the secret compartment below. I stepped back and sat on my bed, breathing slowly, in through my nose, out through my mouth, trying not to throw up. That bottom drawer might seem too shallow to him. He might rap on the bottom, knock the cardboard loose, and find those few black-and-white photographs that he'd missed before. And the Polaroid camera I could use without getting the pictures developed at the store or downloading them on the computer. I felt my knees shaking and clamped my hands over them.

Both my demi-cup bras and the black cotton one went in the garbage bag. I could feel my mother longing to object, seeing as how neither of my parents would want a white bra showing through under a black dress. But Mom held her tongue and the black bra, perhaps a sign of goth tendencies, disappeared into the plastic bag.

My father hesitated in earnest about the pantyhose. My mom stiffened, folded her arms, afraid he would make a mistake and I would be caught in Sunday School with naked legs like some pantheist. But he left the stockings and moved on to the pajamas. He passed over the long-sleeved flannel nightie, but banished the thin white cotton one. He felt the jersey pajamas between his fingers perhaps to test how flimsy they might be. Did he imagine I would answer the door in them some Saturday morning and seduce a Mormon missionary?

He left the pajamas, an innocent color of pale yellow, and moved to the bottom drawer. I held my breath. But all he did, when we saw the mass of mittens, gloves, knit hats, and mufflers, was pull out a black lace shawl. He slid the bottom drawer closed without disturbing the secret chamber.

I was sure it was over, but he stepped to my dressing table and started picking things up. He stole my violet perfume and lifted the lid of my jewelry box. I didn't have pierced ears, so there wasn't a lot to choose from. Still, he took a silver bracelet formed from a row of running figures holding hands, a cheap mood ring, a plain gold anklet chain, a pendant of a pewter feather. He left the crosses and the birthstone hair clip from when I was ten.

I already missed my tank tops, my soft black jacket, but more heartbreaking, he went to my bedside table and unplugged my CD player. I had already learned to check out books I wanted to read from the school library and to leave them in my locker until I returned them. My parents were not novel readers and seemed suspicious of literature. But my music, it was so safe. Words of protest stuck in my throat like clay.

"You can listen to appropriate music in the front room or the family room," he said as he dropped my player in the trash bag, the wires of my earplugs flipping over the rim like spaghetti. "Not alone in your room."

Where I dance naked? I wanted to ask, but I was weak and silent.

He looked at my tiny collection of CDs. Our house was a couple decades behind, when it came to electronics. My father said they were Satan's playthings. The smaller, the more suspicious. So here was my only store of music. And he took everything—the ballet that helped me fall asleep, the Celtic dance music that got me going in the morning, the soundtrack that cheered me up when I closed my eyes and lay under my covers. The beautiful cases clattered into the swelling bag in my father's hand. All my favorite things were being swallowed up.

In my bathroom, he opened the cabinet and started to pick up my mascara.

"She needs to be presentable." My mother finally spoke up.

"She's fifteen. She should not be trying to attract men."

"She can't wear coveralls and wash her hair with a bar of soap," she said, and he must have believed her because he left my toiletries alone.

Again, he did not invite us to follow, but we did. He walked out of the bathroom, down the hall, through the kitchen, into the garage, and up to the garbage can. He lifted the lid, paused to tie a knot in the top of the bag, and gently lowered it into the can, letting the lid fall closed.

The product of my self-expression was not good enough for the Salvation Army. I was already scheming how to get my music back and hide it at school, but the game wasn't over yet.

"Follow me." He was ordering a dog to come. My mother and I sat down obediently in the Prayer Corner.

The spine of the diary crackled as he ripped out a handful of pages and thrust them in front of my face. "Read." When I just stared at the papers he shook them under my nose. "Take them and read."

The pages looked wounded, jagged paper teeth dangling from the left side. The writing at the top of the page started in midsentence so I began with the next paragraph. "I don't know, but I don't think God did that. Not the God I believe in. Could we really worship different Gods?"

My father reached down and tore the page from my grip, jabbed his finger at the next page down. I read out loud from the first line: ". . . dreamed I was walking down a staircase at school and a guy who looked like a guy from that movie we saw in history class walked right up to me and put his hand under my blouse . . ." I hesitated. I remembered the dream, but I couldn't remember how many details I'd written down.

"Go on." My father took his seat now, ready to be entertained. My mother sat with arms folded, legs folded, the foot that wasn't on the floor vibrating as if she were wired to a socket. My vision blurred for a moment — my ears were ringing. I couldn't look at my mother. Something bothered me about the way her foot suddenly stopped shaking.

That was the last thing I remember before I found myself far away: my mother's shoe freezing in midair.

The world disappeared.

⌒

I wasn't in the Prayer Corner anymore. I was sitting on something slanted — birds were chattering away. The shadow of a tree crossed over me . . . no, *through* me. Sunshine and little shadows moved in the breeze. I was sitting on the roof of a house, but not mine. Our roof was flat and covered with white painted gravel—I'd been up there to save a kite once. This roof was covered with brown shingles, the wood all dried out and warped. I recognized our street below. I'd landed two doors down from my house.

Stupidly, the first thing I did when I was free of my life was to fly back to it. When I left the neighbor's roof, I didn't climb down like a human. I floated down like a bird.

I'm dead! I thought. I was as light as smoke. I was sure I must be a ghost. The idea that I might have had a brain aneurysm right in the middle of the Prayer Corner panicked me—I rushed home expecting to hear my mother's screams ring out or sirens to fill the streets, but it was so quiet, you could hear the leaves in the trees fluttering.

I expected to find my body lying on the floor in the family room, though when I flew around the side of our house and stopped at the glass doors, I saw I was wrong.

My parents weren't trying to revive my corpse, because there didn't seem to be anything wrong with me. My body was sitting up straight, my head bowed over my diary. There was a pen in my right hand.

The sliding door was closed, but I could still hear my mother's voice.

"Exodus twenty," she read from the Bible in her lap. "Then God spoke all these words, saying: I am the Lord your God."

The Jenny I used to be took dictation, slowly writing in the journal as my parents watched. Now I noticed there *was* something wrong with me, but nothing my parents could detect.

My flesh was empty. More graceful than a robot from a horror movie, but still horrible.

CHAPTER 2

Jenny

M<small>Y BODY LOOKED HEAVIER TO ME</small>, like a statue of a girl. Maybe my spirit was what gave my flesh and bones their lightness. Since I didn't have any control over my body anymore, it was sickening to watch it move on its own. My hand held the pen, my elbow and shoulder shifted back and forth as I actually wrote in the journal, my eyelids blinked, my head tilted slightly. The worst part was the way my mother and father seemed to have no idea.

Finally my father took the journal from my hands. My back bent forward, feet shifted, as I knelt in the middle of the Prayer Corner. My fingers interlaced, ready for praying, and my parents laid hands on my strange doll head. Why didn't they feel my absence like a chill under their palms? All those things that made me who I was since I was born didn't matter to my parents. I sat outside the glass doors and cried like a baby.

I knew I couldn't take my body with me and I knew I couldn't stay, so without saying goodbye, I abandoned my life. My spirit slid up the wall of my house, rising as slowly as a raindrop in reverse, and glided over the white rocks on our roof. I could see every rotting leaf there as I swam the air over my home and then up high into our neighbor's tree. Like Wendy from *Peter Pan*, I flew through the branches, beyond the leaves, and into the sky.

Was anything possible now? Paris or the pyramids in Egypt? Could I sit on the shoulder of the Statue of Liberty if I wanted? All I knew for sure was that I wanted the opposite of my old life.

My wish was granted — I was there in a single heartbeat.

The painting was huge, three feet wide and six feet high. A girl, probably life size, rode on the back of some half-hidden sea serpent in the middle of an aqua lake. She stood up straight between the monster's fanlike fins and held a glass bowl in her hands. Calmly, as if this kind of thing were totally normal, she poured the water from the bowl into the face of the creature. Her gown was dark blue and fell off one of her white shoulders. Her hair was gypsy black.

But I wasn't like her. Even though it seemed as if no one could see me or hurt me, I was still scared.

A plaque beside the enormous frame said it had been painted by a man named Waterhouse, on loan from Australia. I was in a wing of the county art museum. I'd been there only once, on a school field trip that my parents let me attend because they had been assured there would be no nude statues and because there was an exhibit of artifacts from the Holy Land on display.

But today the walls were full of skin — pale bodies and rich colors. I was surrounded by Pre-Raphaelite paintings from all over the world. A maiden leaned over a balcony to kiss an armored knight, a lady with waves of auburn hair breathed in the scent of a flower in her hand, mermaids lounged around on rocks, water nymphs hid between lily pads and tried to pull a shepherd into their pool. Something my mother would have considered borderline pornography.

I stayed there for I don't know how long before I began to wander and found myself in a wing of photographs. A hundred or more black-and-white pictures surrounded me. No landscapes or bowls of fruit. Every image was human. These were the kinds of photos I'd wanted to take before my parents had shut down my experiments. I stared at the high contrast, deep shade, and blazing light. In one a naked woman lay across a grassy hill, half in and half out of the sun; in the next shadows ran like streams across the speckled skin on the back of a wrinkled hand.

And these weren't just pictures about the beauty of the human body; the spirits looking out of those faces shocked me. An old woman waiting on her porch steps, her eyes heavy with pain. A boy balancing on the bow of a broken rowboat in the sand, flexing his skinny arms and staring down the camera with defiance. They were so fearless about who they were.

⌒

I found out how things worked through trial and error. Sometimes I decided to go somewhere, like when I was back in front of the Waterhouse painting in the blink of an eye because I thought of being there, and other times I found myself in a different place without warning or knowing why.

That's how I landed beside a podium that held an enormous dictionary. I knew the place even though I'd been there only once — the huge main branch library downtown. I came to a story time there with my first grade class.

I moved through the aisles between millions of volumes and realized I could read anything I wanted now, uncensored. It wasn't until I tried to open the cover of a novel on the new arrivals table that I discovered I was wrong. I had to read the back covers of books propped up on book stands and half articles visible on the pages of magazines left open on the couches in the lobby—it was impossible to grasp anything or even turn a page. Eventually I was brave enough to lean over an old man who sat in a study carrel and a woman at the long table in the computer wing and read silently along with them. They weren't reading what I would have chosen myself, but still I liked the quiet and the colors of floor-to-ceiling books.

I visited the dance studio where I'd spent hours taking ballet. I hadn't had lessons in months and I missed it. I loved how the mirrors created a world that went on forever; perfectly matched wooden bars and floors stretched into infinity, with company after company of girls calmly breathing, bending, stretching in unison.

I could see every detail as clearly as if I were lifting onto pointe myself. But I wasn't really there. I proved this to myself by rushing toward the mirrors on the far wall, coming smack up against them without ever appearing in the reflection. I suppose I could have continued on through the mirror, but the idea frightened me.

Once I ended up at the Reed Theater. I stood in the center aisle, a dozen rows from the front, watching *West Side Story*. My parents refused to rent the movie for me; said it was inappropriate. But I had watched it on TV one day when I was home from school with a cold and my mom was at a church committee meeting. I was twelve, and I cried so hard I caught the hiccups.

Now I floated up onto the stage and turned back to see what the audience looked like as Maria and Tony sang a duet. The light from the stage turned everyone into angels—a thousand gold faces in the dark.

I went to a forest many times. There was no sign of human-kind, though there were tiny bugs, camouflaged birds, and chitter-ing squirrels. I darted between tree trunks and leapt over bushes. I jumped streams and climbed to the tops of trees to look down on the forest canopy. I threw myself into the thick of the woods to swing onto a branch and perch there like an elf. Since I weighed nothing I didn't even bend the slenderest twig.

To my surprise, I once found myself back in my old house, in my old bedroom, at my vanity, where the mirrored closet doors behind showed me a view of the empty chair where I sat.

I froze, terrified, not because I wasn't reflected, but because something was moving by the bed. The gentle robot of my body pulled the covers down—I could see it from the corner of my eye. It passed behind me, reflected as a pale apparition I would not focus on. The door swung open and my father said, "Good night, Puppy. Say your prayers."

"Good night, Daddy," said my body.

I hunched down, too afraid to even run away. It was like a scene from one of those old flying saucer movies they showed every Hal-loween. There was nothing creepier than the child who weeps as he tells the policeman, "Those aren't my parents—they look like them, but they're not my mommy and daddy, I tell you! You've got to believe me!" But the policeman never does.

And I was the alien.

That's not me anymore, I told myself. I stood up. *I'm riding a sea serpent.*

And I was back in the museum's Pre-Raphaelite room. But nothing was the same after that. I didn't want to go back to my old life, but my life out-of-body was becoming unsettling. When I went to the dance studio, no boy could be my partner and lift me in a pas de deux, but now I realized that living as a spirit meant no boy would *ever* take me in his arms.

CHAPTER 3

Jenny

I DIDN'T KNOW WHY I FOUND myself in front of that store window with a display of tie-dye kaftans and hemp shirts, but maybe I'd wished for the opposite of my old life. The shop was called Reflections; their logo, made into a stained-glass window in the front door, was a tree of life with a rainbow behind it. My mother refused to go into this or any other New Age store because she was afraid they were fronts for satanic cults.

I slipped right through the door without jingling the tiny string of brass bells that warned the cashier when customers entered. The room was filled with books up to the ceiling, and displays of candles, incense, crystals, massage oils, yoga mats, CDs with monks and angels on the covers, DVDs of Tai Chi masters and pregnant women meditating. Even statues of the Virgin Mary, Saint Francis, Buddha, and a goddess with six arms. There were two customers, an elderly man with glasses pushed low on his nose, and a young woman in overalls who had a sleeping baby strapped to her belly. She chatted with the cashier, a young man wearing black eyeliner and his long hair in a braid.

Even though I felt out of place in this world, the soundtrack that was playing—flute over the sounds of a babbling brook—calmed me. I was attracted to laughter from somewhere beyond the main room of the shop. I drifted back through a grass mat doorway and found a group of seven people sitting in a circle with their eyes closed and their hands in their laps, palms up.

The woman who was speaking seemed the same age as my mother, but she wore her hair in dreadlocks pulled back, and had a single silver stud in one nostril and a tattoo of a flying bird on one wrist. No shoes, no makeup. Like my mom's polar opposite.

"Lift up this picture of your desires to God," she said. "Don't try to figure out how you will receive this gift. Just know that you already have received it and feel the joy. You don't have to know how this blessing will come to be. You only need to be grateful."

Then the woman, who was apparently the leader of the group, stopped and turned her face, eyes still closed, toward me. "Someone's here." She smiled. She opened her eyes for a moment, looked through me, then closed them again. "A spirit has come into the room."

I scanned the room for a strange light or some other sign of the supernatural.

"Is it my father?" one of the others asked. "He died last month." They all stayed still, eyes shut.

I didn't want to see a ghost, so I stopped looking around.

"No," said the leader. "I don't think this person is dead."

I froze. *She means me.* If I moved or breathed she might catch me somehow.

"What?" one of the others whispered. "What did she say?"

"It's nothing to worry about," said the leader. "This soul means no harm. She's just visiting."

"Does she have a message for us?" someone asked.

"Do you have a message for us?" said the leader, looking right at me with her eyes shut.

I said nothing. But I thought, *Please don't talk to me.*

"She's shy," said the leader. "I think she's a little lost."

Childishly I thought, *I know where I am — I just don't want to go home.*

"Oh," the leader laughed. "I stand corrected. She's not lost — she's a bit of a runaway, I think."

Maybe I knew where I was — the street name and which city — but she was right. I *was* lost. I'd gotten stuck in the land of bodiless wandering. I couldn't use a phone or take a drink of water or smell a flower.

"You're welcome here, sweetheart. We won't bother you if you don't bother us. Don't be afraid," said the woman.

But I *was* afraid.

⌐

I started going to Reflections every day at around the same time, just as this woman arrived or sometimes just after she started teaching one of her classes. The second day she seemed surprised when she sensed me watching. The third day, she seemed to expect me. By the fourth she had named me "the Runaway." It was my only pleasure now, having a nickname and being noticed.

I came to sit in the same place every day, on the top of the bookshelf between the two windows. Her name was Gayle. Even though I spent the rest of each day and night alone backstage at the theater or in the arms of a pine tree, I made sure I visited Gayle every day she was there.

"Aren't you ever going home to roost?" she asked me one day.

I'm scared to go home, I thought.

"You're a lonely bird, aren't you?" said Gayle. And then she sang a simple song I'd never heard before—it sounded like a hymn:

> *The lone wild bird in lofty flight*
> *Is still with thee, nor leaves thy sight*
> *For I am thine; I rest in thee;*
> *Great Spirit come and rest in me.*

No one had sung me a lullaby since I was tiny. My mother used to sing me songs about everything we were doing. When she made me a bowl of oatmeal in the morning she'd sing about hungry bear cubs. When she washed behind my ears, leaning over the side of the tub, she would sing about soap bubbles. And when she brushed my wet hair in front of the mirror, she used to press her hand on the back of my neck and comb my curls up over her fingers, singing a song about daisies. I could almost feel the palm of my mother's hand, warm and safe, cupping the back of my head as Gayle sang to me.

And that was the moment I felt *called.*

Every other time I had gone from one place to another, I'd either decided where to fly and swam in the air to the spot, or I'd wished to be somewhere and found myself there. Or I'd appeared in a new setting instantly without knowing why. But now I felt drawn to move in a specific direction as if I were in the blackness of outer space and there was only one star to follow. I flew slowly at first, east, between buildings, then over railroad crossbars and along farm fences. I became more confident and started gaining speed, even though I still had no idea what I was looking for.

It's heading straight for you, I heard some voice inside me whisper.

Instead of scaring me, this only made me want to get there faster. The world rolled forward, the horizon in front of me curling like the crown of an ocean wave. And then, in a rush of magnetic energy, I was swung around and then stopped, hovering in midair. Whatever was coming at me had passed by me, or possibly *through* me. I set my feet down in the grass of an open field where the horizon in every direction was flat. Not a hill or tree to give it shape or size. I had no idea how many miles I'd flown or what state I was in. The heavens came smack down to the earth all around, and I could see the faint curve of the planet in the distance.

But the field wasn't completely empty. About a hundred yards away, I saw a boy levitating three feet off the ground. He came to rest with his sneakers in the grass and walked in my direction as if he'd forgotten he could just fly to me.

CHAPTER 4

Jenny

IN THE MIDDLE OF WHO KNOWS WHERE, in a huge abandoned field, I stood in the grass and watched this boy walk toward me as if it was a perfectly normal way for him to meet a girl.

He strolled right up to me. "Hey."

I wasn't afraid of him, but I felt nervous. "Where did you come from?" I asked.

He gestured with a flick of his head. "That way." Then he smiled. "Is this your place?"

I glanced around to make sure I hadn't imagined where we were standing. "This field?" I said. "Are you asking me if this is *my* empty field?"

He shrugged, looked me up and down. I scanned my feet, my hands and arms, and I could see myself but I wasn't sure if he viewed me the way I did. And I was too embarrassed to ask him what I looked like. In my own eyes I wore jeans and a white T-shirt and, strangely, the soft black jacket my father had thrown out. Even stranger, my feet were bare.

"Are you dead?" he asked.

"What?" It seemed almost insulting. Did I look like a corpse? "No." I thought I knew how these things worked. The spirits I had seen on my travels weren't ghosts—they were people out of their bodies temporarily. "You're not dead, are you?"

"Maybe," he said.

"Do you remember dying?" I asked.

He put his hands in his pockets. He wore jeans too, with a black shirt rolled at the sleeves and open at the throat. But he had the good sense to be wearing sneakers.

"I don't want to remember that." His face went gray and he held out a hand as if he wanted to protect himself from me.

And then he was gone.

Weird. I just stood there, doing nothing, for a long time. He was a stranger—it would be impossible for him to hurt my feelings. I couldn't miss him, seeing as how I'd only known him for a few seconds. It wasn't as if he had made me doubt the truth—*I* wasn't dead. And neither was he: he just didn't know it. What was it that bothered me about him?

I sat down on the grass and replayed our conversation. I couldn't figure out why we had looked at each other and spoken to each other when I hadn't been noticed by any of the other souls I saw floating outside their bodies: an old woman napping in a wheelchair while her spirit danced around her, a man meditating on the beach with his spirit levitating a foot over his head. They hadn't seen me.

And what made this boy and me fly toward each other literally out of the blue? It felt as if we'd been running along trying to launch kites and then our strings got tangled and swung us back toward each other.

But what were the kites we were hanging on to?

I realized why I missed him—he could see and hear me, and it was almost like being real again. But there was nothing I could do about it—he'd run away. I finally got myself up and went to some of my favorite locations: museum, beach, theater. But by the next day, I had to return to that field. It was haunting me.

But why would *he* be back? What were the chances that he was still thinking about me?

Then he dropped down out of the air and went into a skydiver roll a dozen feet away from me. He brushed himself off, an unnecessary gesture that cracked me up, but I wouldn't let myself be charmed. I didn't trust him yet. Hadn't he said I looked dead and then run away?

"You don't think I'm a ghost?" he asked, as if our previous conversation were still on the table.

"I don't think I can see ghosts," I explained. "Only spirits." He waited for more. "Spirits on vacation from their bodies," I explained. "You know, not done with their bodies."

"Like when someone's asleep?" he asked.

"Or meditating."

He strolled up a little closer. "Which one are you?"

"None of the above. I just left my body, you know, like breaking out of prison."

"What made your body a prison?" he asked me. When I didn't answer right away he lifted one eyebrow. In another setting it would have been cute, but everything about him was annoying me for some reason.

"You don't want to know," I said.

"Yes, I do."

"Well, I don't want to tell you."

"No questions about the past. I get it," he said. "If I'm not dead," he went on, "I guess this isn't heaven."

"No." More like hell, I wanted to say, but why spoil his fun. Maybe he was still rejoicing in his freedom the way I had at first.

"Well, it can't be hell." He gestured at me as if I were proof of that. "Is it like a parallel universe?"

That didn't sound good. Too much like purgatory. I felt a ripple of fear spread through me. Maybe it felt like hell because it *was* hell.

"It's the same world as before," I insisted, trying to convince myself. "Just the outside edge. My house is the same. All the street signs have the same names." It was scaring me, the idea that he might be right, that we were in some kind of limbo. "Didn't you see your house and family after you left your body?"

I could see the tension of his own story behind his eyes, but he didn't share it. "Sorta like there's safety glass between us and everything else," he said. To test the rules, he reached out and took my hand. I jumped but didn't pull away. The warmth of his fingers fascinated me. But I wasn't sure if I was feeling his hand or the energy of his hand. Or the heat of his *thinking* of my hand in his.

He let go. "No wall between us, though."

My blush throbbed hot like a bad sunburn even though I technically had no skin. "I didn't say you could touch me."

"Sorry . . ." He paused. "What's your name?"

The idea of telling him my name and where I lived and what made me leave my body, the idea of explaining about my parents, made my stomach go cold. Again, no organs. Why could I still feel emotions forming in those parts of me I'd left behind?

"I forgot," he said. "No questions about the past." He smiled. "So if this isn't your field, why do you come here?"

To find you, stupid, I thought. Before I landed in the field, I'd been racing toward something I couldn't name — a boy I couldn't name. If he hadn't felt the same force I had, throwing us at each other, maybe that wasn't real.

I felt deflated, but I told him the truth. "I was rushing toward something — you, I guess. I only stopped here because that's where I found myself when I passed you going the other way."

He thought for a moment. "I thought I saw my shadow on the ground. That never happened before. Like the shadow of a bird on the ground before it lands, only the shadow wasn't bigger than me and it wasn't getting smaller when I got closer." He looked uncertain. "I guess that was you."

A chill fluttered up what would've been my neck.

"You're the only other ghost I've seen," he told me.

"I'm not a ghost." Odd that he hadn't seen one single other person out of body. "Where do you usually hang around?"

"Sand dunes and caves. The ocean. The mountains."

He didn't travel populated areas — maybe he was a beginner. "How long have you been out of body?"

"I don't count sunsets," he said. "I chase them sometimes. Think I could ever make time go backwards?"

He was so immature. "No."

"But if I flew so fast toward the sunset that I passed it, wouldn't it be up in the sky again? Would I be hours back?" He studied my face and throat. "Let's say I flew three hours backwards. Why can't I fly ten times faster and get to yesterday?"

"Go ahead." I smirked at him. "I'll wait here."

He grinned and flew away so quickly that I could hardly make out the blur of his black shirt, like a faint storm cloud against the sky. Then nothing, as if he'd never been there at all.

The wind still shifted the grass and there was the distant cry of a crow somewhere, the tick of a beetle, but otherwise silence.

I did not miss him. How could I? Our two conversations still totaled less than ten minutes. It was ridiculous. But the idea of leaving our field depressed me. I couldn't imagine a single inspiring place to visit.

Irritating as he was, I wanted him to come back, but there were no stars out yet for making wishes. It was almost sunset, though. How many hours had passed?

Like a sneak attack, he rushed at me from the side and threw his arms around me, sending me into the grass. He rolled away laughing. The tingle of his touch vibrated up and down and all through me, cold and warm at the same time.

"Did it work?" He sat up. "Do you remember me or is it yesterday?"

I acted without thinking. I sped away, wanting to get back at him. I went to a cliff I'd been to many times. It was twilight there already, and the forest below was dim — only the mountain across the valley still glowed pink from the sunset. It made me smile, thinking of him standing there in the field alone. The same way he'd left me.

But as the light crept away, I started to realize that I might never see him again. How could I find him? Even if I raced around the globe at light speed, the chance of crossing paths with him again might be microscopic. And it wasn't as if I could go back to my body and look him up in the phone book. I didn't know his name or what part of the world he lived in. The only thing connecting us was that stretch of grass.

When I came back to the field, the sky was turning a deep shade of purplish blue. I walked around pretending that his absence didn't hurt. The way the grass refused to part for me, no matter how I kicked as I passed through, made me mad. I walked in smaller and smaller wheels, and if I'd been solid I bet I would've made a spiral crop circle — finally I lay down on my back as the stars came out. I don't think I could've been lonelier if I'd been on Jupiter.

"Hey."

My joy was offset by the look on his face. Zero recognition. He knelt, leaning over me and smiling.

"Who are you?" he asked.

CHAPTER 5

Jenny

H<small>E DIDN'T REMEMBER ME</small>! I sat up, speechless. And he sat back, laughing.

"Just kidding," he said. "I was going to pick you some flowers, but it didn't work."

"How did you know I'd still be here?"

"Hmmm." He looked me up and down.

"Do you think you're that irresistible?"

"Hey," he said. "I tried to pick you flowers and now you're making fun of me."

The field was dark. I shouldn't have been able to see anything. But there were his eyelashes catching the starlight and the white of his teeth as he smiled and a strand of his hair moving in the breeze. We were seeing each other with our minds, I supposed, instead of eyes. "Really, how did you know I'd be here?"

"You didn't say goodbye," he said with a shrug. "And you seem like a nice person, like someone who would at least leave a note if you were never coming back."

I tried not to look disappointed, but having a boy think you're nice usually means he thinks of you as a sister. I didn't have to be that sisterly girl. He didn't know anything about the old me. It was like I always hoped college would be someday—a new beginning. A place you can create yourself from scratch and start over.

"Okay." I still didn't trust him. There must be some catch. He was talking to me—most boys didn't. And he was cute. "I could've left without saying goodbye," I told him.

"Yeah?"

"I left my old life without saying goodbye," I said, but then I felt bad because he looked sort of haunted.

"So did I," he said.

Maybe he had someone who would miss him. I bet his family would notice if an empty body was walking around like a robot all of a sudden.

"You didn't have to come back just to say goodbye to me," he said. "You're free to do whatever you want."

"I know." I tried to fake indifference. "It's not like we're friends. We just met." But I was trying too hard—he could tell I was glad he'd come back.

"You're my only spirit friend," he said. "There's no one else to talk to." Then he held up a hand. "That sounded bad. I meant, even if there was a hundred spirits standing around here, I'd want to talk to you."

Again, how could I blush? "'My only spirit friend'? Are you a third-grader?"

"We said we weren't gonna talk about our pasts, including what grade I'm in or if I'm flunking out. That was then. Now I'm a su-perhero. I can fly, and dematerialize, and I'm working on turning back time."

It was funny that he thought being out of body made him powerful, because most of the time it made me feel powerless. I couldn't move a blade of grass or be heard by anyone no matter how loud I yelled in their ears; I couldn't even make a shadow in the blazing sun. I felt just as trapped in this out-of-body world as I had in the old one. But he was right — we could fly. That had always been at the top of my wish list when I was little.

"Where did you fly to when you left me?" I asked.

"I went to this coral reef I like and jogged around awhile, and then when you left me I went to this park near where I used to live, but I couldn't steal any of the roses."

He didn't wait in the field when I flew away from him. I felt a little hurt, but I also admired his self-confidence. And he'd thought of roses. "You jogged around a coral reef?" I asked. "On top of the coral?"

"No, it's under water."

At first I didn't get it, but then I realized the weight of the water wouldn't slow him down. He could run on the sea floor as easy as he could've run down the sidewalk when he was in his body. "I haven't tried that," I said.

"Yet."

"Yet." I smiled.

"Under water is really cool. And running on the surface is fun too." He demonstrated by jogging around me in a circle, dipping down into the earth so that only his head and shoulders showed, and then back up again. I guess I looked surprised because he said, "You could run through a mountain, if you want — it's dark, but it's not like it hurts or makes you tired." He nodded at my clothes. "Won't even get your dress dirty."

I was shocked to find I was wearing a party dress that I'd never owned or even seen before, as far as I knew—rose pink. And still I was barefoot. My mind had conjured up clothes without my permission. Was there something about him that made me want to look more girlish?

He sat beside me. "Where did *you* go?"

"A cliff," I said. It sounded so boring.

"When you jump from here to some other place, can you go anywhere, or do you have to have a place in mind?" he asked.

"Sometimes I picture a kind of place, like I'd think of pine trees, and then I'd be in a forest," I told him.

"At first I thought I had to have been to a place before if I wanted to land there, but then I decided to try to go somewhere famous I'd never been, and zap, I was right there. It was freaky."

"Like where?" I felt a lift inside me, as if the crest of a wave were taking me up for a moment.

"I went to the pitcher's mound of Yankee Stadium." He counted on his fingers so as not to miss any of the really good ones. "The top of Mount Everest. The Hollywood sign."

This started to feel like a dream. Not just the crazy things we were discussing, but the way he was looking at me. Guys at school never flirted with me.

"Do you have to know what it looks like? I mean, you've seen pictures of the Hollywood sign," I said. "Or can you just make up a spot? Let's say one mile directly east of where I'm standing?"

He shrugged. "Try it." When I hesitated, he said, "I won't ditch you. I promise."

So I decided to go and was suddenly sitting in the same position, but in a brushy patch of weeds beside a wire fence. I looked west, but there must've been a slight rise in the land between me and our field — I couldn't see him in the distance. I zapped back to where I'd been.

"I think it worked," I told him. "But it's not like I walked back and measured the distance."

He got up on his knees. "Okay, I'm going to visit the spot on the exact opposite of the globe from right here."

He didn't worry that I would ditch him, apparently. He disappeared in a blink and was back five seconds later. "You're right. Hard to prove I did that correctly," he said. "It was — "

"No, don't tell me what it looked like." I smiled. "We'll both decide to go to the spot exactly on the other side of the earth and see if we end up in the same place."

He grinned. "One, two, three."

Strangely, we sat facing each other on the moving back of the oceans. There was no land in sight and only starlight glimmering off the constantly appearing and vanishing edges of waves.

I felt a laugh building in my middle. He pointed at me and we zipped back to the field. This zapping back and forth in space would've seemed like a dream, but I'd never had a dream this interesting.

"What if you want to go somewhere that's not familiar to me, like the playground of the school where you went to kindergarten, or your grandma's back porch?" I asked. "You could find it but I'd be lost, right?"

He shrugged. "It's not like you'd really be lost," he said. "You could just decide to come back to this field."

"Okay." It couldn't actually be dangerous. We couldn't be hurt. And he was right—all I'd have to do was fly to a place I was familiar with. "Pick somewhere only you know."

He thought for a second. "How about the park where I learned to ride a two-wheeler?"

"Sure."

"Wait." He looked anxious for a moment. "I don't want to be able to take you somewhere you don't want to go."

"If I don't like it, I'll zip right out of there," I told him.

He thought about that for a few seconds. "I guess." He shrugged. "Okay. But you go first. You take me somewhere."

"The first beach I ever went to," I said aloud.

In a flash I was standing knee-deep in waves at Archer Beach—the water couldn't wet my dress or pull on my legs, but I was there. Only, I was alone. I could see a lonely parking lot light on the hill nearby, a log in the sand that looked a bit like a crocodile in the moonlight. I paused, to make sure he wasn't going to pop out of the water and surprise me.

When I came back to the field he was right beside me and said, "Guess that doesn't work."

"Maybe I have to really take you." I reached over and took his hand. The heat made something curl inside me.

This time I thought of a place he would not know or think of as significant. I didn't even say it out loud. I just thought of the department store window where as a little girl I'd stared at a ballet scene from *Giselle* displayed in marionettes. After that day, I wanted to be a ballerina.

Even though we weren't reflected in the glass, we stood on the sidewalk inches from the windowpane, and I still held his hand.

"Shit," he whispered, looking around—he gripped my hand tight. "That's freaky." Then he corrected himself. "Freakier."

We tested several theories. For one of us to take the other to an unfamiliar place, we had to be touching. We found by trial and error that if we chose a famous place but did not get specific, and did not hold hands, we'd sometimes end up far away from each other: one below the letters of the Hollywood sign and the other on top, or on two different sides of Niagara Falls. To stay together we had to touch. When we were arm in arm or hand in hand, either of us could say or think a place and we'd fly there, as fast as a thought.

Standing face-to-face, holding each other by both hands, we took turns naming places, faster and faster. As soon as I realized we were standing between the paws of the Sphinx in Egypt, I would say, "The Lincoln Memorial," and we'd be in Washington, D.C., standing on the stone steps with a giant looking down on us. We never felt the heat of the volcano in Hawaii or smelled the beasts in the darkened lion cage at the Bronx Zoo, but the colors and the light—and the strange sounds—it was amazing.

Even so, even with the beauty of the view from Mount Rushmore and the stars above us in the Yosemite Valley and the foggy view from the Golden Gate Bridge, I stopped staring at the scenery.

It was fascinating how his face was a constant—the lighting changed the shadows and lit his features in different colors, but his gaze on me was unshakable.

"The Great Wall of China," I said, and around us a gray ribbon of stone materialized like the arching back of a dragon. I could see the tiny reflection of it in his eye. I looked closer to see if I could find myself reflected there, but I could never get quite close enough.

"Caesar's Palace in Las Vegas," he said, and an enormous fountain appeared in a golden glowing hotel lobby.

"Beautiful." I asked, "If you hadn't said 'Las Vegas,' would we be in Rome right now?"

He laughed. A small dog came by in the arms of an elderly woman—when it kept its gaze on him and began to growl, he growled back and the pitiful thing ducked into the armpit of its owner.

"That was weird," he said. "Are you sure I'm not a ghost?"

"The stage of Ford's Theatre," I whispered. Everything went black and the only way I knew we were in a darkened theater was that an amber safety bulb backstage illuminated the bars of lights and loops of ropes forty feet above us. His face was in the dark, but his hair was lit from above. Or did I just imagine that?

"The Sea of Tranquility," he whispered. We were in a chalk gray landscape with an ink black sky. His face half-lit made me wish I had a camera. Would he show up on film? Then I noticed the earth hanging in the sky in crisp blue, black, and white. The idea of being on the moon frightened me. I closed my eyes and he laughed at me.

We were not solid, but we could touch each other, see each other, and definitely we could feel each other. When he took my face in his hands and gave my head a playful shake, I felt as if I were spinning around until I fell down, just like I had when I was a little girl. He was smiling. In return I gave him a gentle push on the shoulder, and from my fingertips, up my arms, all through me, I buzzed with the pleasure—like swinging on a playground swing, that weightless joy at the far end of each sweep. That was how I felt, as if I was always moving toward him and away from him and back to him again.

"Your turn," he said.

"The Eiffel Tower," I whispered. Iron lace towered upward.

"The crazy cars at Fun Zone," he said.

I took one look at the spinning faces, laughing tourists circling us in a blur, then closed my eyes again, holding on to him for balance. His arms folded me into his energy, our combined spirits making their own electric charge.

The speed of our game was getting to me. Maybe he sensed this, because he asked, "Should we slow things down?"

"Yes."

"Hollywood Wax Museum," he said.

The museum was closed — it was almost pitch-black, but there was just enough light from an exit sign to make out a row of figures looming over us, one directly beside us. A faint glint in the unblinking eyes was eerie enough, but I could also make out the unhealthy camel color of the wax cheeks and the frozen smile of Dorothy from *The Wizard of Oz*. She stood right at my left shoulder. We were standing with the Lion and the Tin Man and the Scarecrow — there was a painting of the Emerald City behind their heads. That storybook setting should have made them seem friendly, but I felt small and terrified. It wasn't the texture of Dorothy's cheek or the disturbingly permanent wave of her hair that made me feel sick. It was imagining sitting in front of a mirror and looking into her eyes and maybe in my closet door seeing the back of her head.

I felt guilty about being horrified. I should have sent us to some flowery hilltop, but my thoughts had taken a dive.

"Do you think we could go to places we didn't want to go?" he asked. Reading my mind again.

"I don't know." I didn't want to experiment anymore. "Why?"

"Who is in charge, your brain or your emotions?"

"I don't want to play that game," I said.

"Where would you not want to go?" he asked me.

"No," I said. But it was too late.

CHAPTER 6

Jenny

T HAT PARTICULAR LIGHT AT THE BOTTOM of the door was too familiar. I heard the hallway creaking the way it did when my father walked toward the family room.

Why was I like this? Dorothy would have loved coming back to Kansas for a moment and catching a glimpse of her aunt. But all I wanted was to go back to Oz.

Back to the field, I thought. But we were still in my darkened bedroom. The light from the hall poured in through my door as it opened partway. The two of us cast no shadows, of course.

I looked away as my father looked in and then closed the door again. I didn't want to see him. Or my mother. But it was the idea of seeing my own body lying in bed that turned my heart to ice.

"Is this your house?" he asked.

But all I could say was "Let's go."

"It looks nice," he said. "What's wrong with it?"

I could hear my father and mother talking in the office. The words were muffled, but there was something about the way he talked over her, and the soothing tone he used, that depressed me. I wanted my mother to have the last word for a change, but she went silent.

"I want to leave," I said.

He took my wrist, held it hard. And we were thankfully away from there. We stood in a gloomy hallway with barred cells along one wall. I could hear the sounds of prisoners, a cough, a low voice talking, perhaps reading aloud, someone snoring, someone else tapping softly, a nervous habit.

"Is this where you don't want to be?" I asked.

He didn't answer, just stared down the corridor.

"I don't want to play anymore," I told him. I gripped his shoulders and gave him a shake as I wished us back to the field, but my hand slipped off him at the last moment and I was in the field alone. I turned around and around—he didn't come back with me.

Take me to the place I was standing right before this, I thought. And I was back in the prison. But he wasn't.

"Take me to *him*," I said out loud, and I was instantly in a hospital corridor. I peeked into the closest room. It was dark. All I could see was that a woman lay in the hospital bed with only her pale arm and hand visible, lit by the nurse call button on the side of the bed rail.

Maybe I shouldn't have been able to find him that way. I don't know why I could. But he was sitting on the floor against the side of the bed. He jumped up, furious.

"How did you get here?"

"I don't know. I said I wanted to go to you."

"I don't want you here." He stood between me and the woman patient.

"What's so terrible about visiting someone in the hospital?" I asked. "That's a nice thing to do."

But his fury flared up and he grabbed my wrist. "Field!" As

soon as we were there he let go of me. No, he didn't just release my wrist — he threw it out of his hand.

"I'm sorry," I stammered.

"You think I want you to follow me into a place like that?"

I could feel him about to disappear. "Wasn't that the point of the game?" I asked. It was so frustrating to be in trouble when I hadn't done anything wrong. I'd had enough of that for one lifetime.

"Stay away from me," he said.

"No, *you* stay away from *me*," I told him. "This is my field."

"Bullshit."

"I was here first!" I yelled at him. "You get out!"

"I don't take orders from you!" he yelled back. "I can go anywhere I want."

"Well, so can I!" I wanted to throw something at him. I hurled a fistful of nothing at his face.

He flinched as if I'd slapped his cheek and I was instantly sorry. He wouldn't look me in the eye — he flew backwards away from me in a flash and was gone.

I hated that I had lashed out at him, and I missed him so hard, I wished I knew his name so I could scream it. I wanted to rewind our fight and take back my words.

I used to think I was always in trouble with my parents because their rules were so strict, but here was my first new relationship and I had killed it already. I sat down in the grass and cried.

"Okay," I heard him say. "We'll share it." He stood over me with his hands on his hips. "You can have this side of the field and I'll take the other." With his foot he drew a line on the ground that made no impression in the grass. "Deal?"

I was glad to have him back, more than I was willing to admit to him, but I still felt unlovable. He lay down on the ground just on the other side of the invisible line, his arms folded across his chest.

"Shouldn't sharing be like both of us enjoying the whole field?" I asked.

"It's sharing like I break my cookie in half and give you one of the pieces."

I lay down on my own side inches away from him. "No, my cookie and I give half to you."

He moved closer to me, fitting his shoulder, arm, hip, and leg up against me in such a comfortable way, I worried again that his attraction to me might be brotherly. "Same difference," he said.

The night was deep, the stars had risen, a faint glow defined every blade of grass. Wasn't it strange that the stars sparkled in his eyes even though he would not cast an image in a mirror himself? When I looked up, the heavens seemed so big, I almost felt like I was falling into them.

"Let's just forget what we saw," I whispered. "I can't even re-member where I found you."

"Okay." His arms relaxed.

"Did I hurt you?" I asked, turning to see if his face was marked.

"No," he said, but I wasn't so sure.

I pushed up even closer to him—arms, sides, hip to hip, legs, even our feet, his right and my left, pressed together. He lifted his foot and rested it over my ankle, gently pinning me down.

Then he pointed into the heavens. "Want to go there?"

"Where?"

"That star." He gave his finger an extra stretch toward the doz-ens of stars in that general direction. "The one by those other two stars."

"What do you mean?" I lifted my arm so it was touching his, our hands and fingers aligned, and pointed. "That one?"

"No," he complained. Then he swiped his fingers across our view of the sky, like he was flicking away a speck of dust or a drop of water, and the night surged forward. The stars, staying perfectly aligned, curved across the sky — time had sped into the future an hour.

I gasped at this and grabbed his hand, pulling it back toward our bodies as if he might accidentally throw the earth off its rotation. The stars slowed again, appearing to have stopped.

"How did you do that?" I whispered.

"I took us somewhere we hadn't been yet," he said. "Forward in time."

He said it so matter-of-factly, but the idea made me shiver on the inside.

"Just a little," he reassured me.

"That's . . . so cool." I pointed at one particularly bright star and gave it a push with my fingertip in the air. The map of stars glided forward again, constellations staying aligned as they grace-fully passed over us, not a long way, just a bit into the tail of the night, an hour or two closer to morning.

He made a sound of alarm, a fake cry, and then laughed. "Here." He lifted his arm to mine, our hands together, our index fingers pointing up. As one, without saying aloud what we would do, we moved the stars a few minutes westward, then froze. "Look what we can do together," he said.

"What did we do?"

"We stopped time," he whispered.

I didn't believe him at first. I watched the star at the end of my finger for a long while. He just lay there waiting for me to admit it. "Did we really?" I asked.

"We pooled our superstrength."

"So you think I couldn't have done it by myself?" I teased him.

"Okay." He withdrew his hand and folded him arms over his chest again. "Now you're just getting power hungry."

Of course we hadn't truly stopped planets and suns in the vacuum of space—I supposed we had stopped our perception of time. Which was just as magic.

The warmth of his spirit along the side of mine made me bold. I pointed both my hands toward the east and swept my arms westward. As the night sky appeared to fly by, and the sun raced up the ceiling of purple, brightening it to blue, as clouds sailed over us, scudding along, he slid between my open arms and kissed me.

I'd never been kissed, so I had nothing to compare it with. We had eyes to see and we could hold hands, and I supposed we had lips, because we kissed. But I also knew we were out of our bodies. So how was it that he tasted like rain? It was dizzying how we could press into each other further than humans ever could. He was pulling something out of me, like my sense of balance—he was dropping me off a cliff and I never wanted him to let go.

But it was also disturbing. How would we ever sort ourselves out from each other again?

The heavens were still floating along, faster than they should. I didn't know how many days had rolled past. I shot my hand up and slowed down the sun halfway up the sky. Maybe time didn't mean anything to us anymore, but if flinging the stars around shortened the number of minutes I had with him, I needed to put the planets back in rhythm. How many times had the moon crossed over us while we were kissing?

He had made the world of wandering spirits safe for me. But again came that nagging feeling that there was something wrong. We'd never be able to eat in a restaurant together. We'd never have our picture taken in a photo booth. He'd never pick me up in a car. I'd never make him a birthday cake.

A random cloud muted the light and I felt the heaviness of my old life pushing down on me, a lead coat I wanted to shrug off.

"If we're dreaming," I asked him, "do you think one of us might wake up by accident?"

"What are you talking about?" He smiled.

"One day I saw a baby napping and its spirit was three feet away from its body, but then it woke up and the baby ghost disappeared."

"The spirit disappeared?"

"No, I mean, its spirit went back into the body. But if I'd been looking at just the spirit, you know, it would have seemed like it vanished."

"Are you worried I'll disappear?" he asked.

"I don't know." I felt embarrassed to have brought it up. "I felt like I almost got sucked back to my old life a couple of times, but you're probably not going anywhere. I mean, you could be in a coma."

He sat up. "Why did you say that?"

He was angry again. It stung tears into my eyes. "I didn't mean anything bad." He still looked so dark—I'd damaged him some-how. "I don't know what I'm talking about," I said. "Don't listen to me."

"I can't stay here." He stood up.

"I take it back," I said, scrambling to my feet. "What did I do?"

He seemed far away—I couldn't quite reach him.

"Aw, shit," he sighed.

"Where are you going?" I reached for him. "I'll go with you!" My fingers gripped his shirt.

For one moment we were both on a city bus. He was staring at a boy and girl sitting across the aisle. I wanted to look at them too, but a man was standing between us. Was that boy him? Or his body?

Everything was blurry. My hand slipped off his sleeve and I was in the field again, fallen in the grass. He came back, but it was as if he was a faded picture of himself.

"You can't come with me." He knelt beside me—his voice wavered like a blowing leaf twisting in and out of the light. I tried to take his hand but I couldn't seem to.

"Why do you have to leave?" I asked.

His face, like his voice, was getting lost in waves of shadow and sunshine. "Listen," he said, and then he told me his name aloud. The words, though, curled and evaporated in the air before I could catch them. Then he was telling me a street name. And a list of numbers so I could find him.

I threw myself toward him, stretching out to try to put my arms around him, but there was nothing to hold on to. He was there and then not and there again. His mouth was moving. I couldn't read lips, but I thought he said someone was crying.

"Who is crying?" I asked him. But my words were coming apart. My voice turned to colors and tastes and scents instead of sounds. Blue and salty tears and fresh grass. I tried to tell him my name, the street where I lived, but my words and the numerals of my phone number turned into dust and flew off on the wind. What I thought were his eyes in the fluttering light were just flashes of sun reflecting off the blowing specks of my voice.

The breeze calmed and the face of the sun was clear again. I was alone. I tried to remember every detail I could about his face and the tone of his voice. I tried to remember everything he'd said to me. I was sure there were clues there that would help me find him.

A sound vibrated through me like a note played on a cello, low and sad, and then the bow lifted off the string and there was silence.

I had just been trying to remember something about a field.

Now someone was pounding on the door.

PART 2

CHAPTER 7

Helen

STRANGE HOW MANY THINGS CAN frighten a ghost. Staring down
at a body I had so recently possessed, for one. Knowing that the
choices I had made while I occupied it would take a heavy toll on
its rightful owner—that was another.

I felt that I had lived for many days in heaven, but it looked to
me as if on earth the Quick had been suspended in time. Apparently for Jenny, less than a minute had passed since I left her. She
was still in the bathtub where I'd stepped out of her body and she
had slipped into it again. She was shivering and naked like a newly
born creature, the water swirling 'round her and down the drain.

I realized, as I stood beside her bathroom sink, that I was
mistaken. Somehow I had returned to visit her *before* I last left
her—the shock of this went up through my spirit like a mouse up
a bell cord. I knew that time was not strictly linear, as the Quick
measure it. But arriving before I'd left should have been impossible.

Jenny seemed unaware of being observed. She breathed un-
evenly and wiped wet strands of hair from her face. How odd that I
was the one who commanded that hand moments ago.

Now that I was back in the land of the Quick, heaven seemed
like something I must've dreamed. Yet I knew I had been there

with James. Some things, for instance—who were guests at the great feast—I noticed had already been lost in crossing back into the world of the Quick. Other things—the way leaves floated down gently onto the linen tablecloth, the smell of fresh bread, and the simple beauty of a bowl of magnolia blossoms—these images were still bright in my mind.

Heaven was real.

I didn't think James would understand, which is why I hadn't said goodbye. The idea had come to me in a rush—I knew that I had to go back to earth and find Jenny. One does not abandon a child in a storm. I was determined to stay with the girl until the wrong I had done her had been righted. Just a short time. Then I would go back to him.

Heaven is not a place you leave behind carelessly—I wanted to stay, of course. And I would have thought it a great struggle to return to the earth, but for me the crossing was easy.

As I focused on the last place I had seen Jenny, I found I was on a road, but still in heaven. I strode to the point of convergence between my pathway and the first row of trees, then pictured Jenny's face. Not my reflection in a mirror when I was inside her, and not her empty shell before I stole her flesh, but her wet, bewildered eyes just after she had reclaimed her body. I saw those curved lashes and her pale face and neck, her round ears, her pointed chin.

There was a kind of flattening then, as if the road and the woods were drawn on a piece of paper and some unseen hand had turned the page away from me, foreshortening the landscape. The folding, inky bridge to Jenny pressed me like the claustrophobic moment when you try to pull a too-tight dress off over your head and it catches at the ribs. I drew myself in and pushed through.

Everything beyond was blinding white: white walls, white tiles. And there she was, waiting in the water.

The bath had drained out and the tap was pouring water down over Jenny's feet. She was quivering and pale, but her cheeks were flushed as she took in her surroundings — the sweater lying on the floor, the empty prescription bottle, the scattering of sleeping pills.

Most of her troubles were ones I had brought to her when I'd stolen her body. In my defense, she had left it empty, but that was no excuse — I was a thief. For the chance to be a solid, living girl again, I had taken up the shell of this fifteen-year-old. At a church picnic, no less, as she sat with head bowed in prayer. Every time I remembered this, it shamed me. The fact that I was in love at the time and that borrowing a body was the only way to touch James, skin to skin, made it no less wicked.

I had been Light, dead and bodiless, for more than a century before I laid eyes on Jenny. When I slid my spectral fingers into her folded hands and breathed through the instrument of her ribs and belly for the first time, I wept with joy.

How strange that after waiting a hundred and thirty years for a body, I kept hers for only six days. For less than a week I played the part of Jenny. Slept in her bed, answered to her name. I'd shocked her family and friends, said and done things Jenny never would have. I inadvertently brought accusations against an honorable man. I bedded James using Jenny's body without permission and then left her alone and unprotected with no memory of the days I had lived as her. I owed her my protection and loyalty now.

The girl jumped at the sound of the doorbell. What was about to happen both thrilled and worried me. I had seen part of what was coming already. Forgetting the obvious, I reached for a towel to wrap around her, but my fingers passed through the cloth. I'd imagined exactly how to protect her, fashioned a detailed plan in my mind as I traveled back to earth. How could I help if I couldn't even make the towel tremble when I swiped at it?

Jenny was about to be thrown into great difficulties, all my doing, all while her spirit had been away on some mysterious adventure I knew nothing about.

Watching her cower in that porcelain coffin brought me back to my last day as one of the Quick. And that's where every ghost story begins, with a death.

⌒

I didn't know I was about to die, of course, but even so, my last day held a strange undercurrent that began with first light. The air smelled familiar, although I couldn't place the scent. I was sitting in the rocker, holding my sleeping baby, as the sun rose with an ominous hue. I wondered if a neighboring farm was on fire, but I smelled no smoke and I'd heard no warning bells or cries for help.

My husband walked past us, displeased with me, as usual, because he thought my answering our daughter's cries in the night would spoil her. But his coldness toward her made me want to comfort her more. If I could have climbed into her cradle, I would've made it my nightly refuge—we were each other's favorite and only companions.

On my last day, I knew something was not right. Something was approaching—either dangerous, like a storm, or wonderful, like a gift by post. Or better, a sea voyage, an adventure to rival the novels I read again and again. The excitement that was hiding behind the foreboding sunrise, the possibility of a marvelous change, some new opportunity, was the only reason I agreed when my husband said he would be away from home all day. We didn't need protecting, so I thought.

As I baked the morning biscuits, the screen door creaked but did not open, dust devils danced at the foot of the porch, and the light became more and more queer. The air was thick and yellowed. As my husband walked out of the house, I looked out through the lace curtains to catch the last glimpse of him. He took our mare, but not the wagon. I saw his broad back in a white shirt, his hair blowing as he rode bareheaded through our gate and away.

It wasn't until that moment, when the weathervane above us squealed to change position, that I recognized the smell of that morning: It was the scent of a mountain of unshed rain. So it was a storm that was coming after all. Uncommonly big, perhaps, but just rain. No impending miracle on the horizon. A bad rain would mean lots of work cleaning up afterward. But I tried to cheer myself — my husband was gone for the day and that freedom always lightened my heart. We had the house to ourselves.

The weather continued to vex us with peculiar scents, vibrations, and utterances. The windows rattled as if some invisible hand played them with a fiddle bow. On the bulging black horizon, flashes bounced like fireflies in the dark cupped hands of the sky.

I took out a bowl and pan, but before I had even scooped out the flour for the cookie dough, the wind that leaked through the windowpane seams blew a puff of white powder off the top of the sack like a tiny specter. I lifted my child out of the wooden highchair and left the kitchen. As I passed through the dining room, the lace cloth on the table was rippled by some mysterious draft.

I headed upstairs with the idea that I would sit in bed with the baby in my lap and the blankets over our heads, but was stopped by a crash, then the sound of breaking glass. A gust of cold air swept over us—a second-floor window must have broken. A branch from our oak tree had probably smashed into one of the bedroom casements. My daughter whimpered and clung to me mightily. I stopped with my feet on two different steps.

I returned to the lower of the steps—should I go up and try to save certain treasures from the rain? The two nice pictures we had in frames on the dresser—a portrait of my parents and a tintype of my husband as a boy? My grandmother's christening gown, folded in paper and sprinkled with dried lavender in the cedar chest, should be safe. But my books—I should hurry and save them.

Or should I run downstairs with my girl and close us into the cellar?

If the winds became a tornado, that would be the safest place to hide. The whole house could rip out at the foundations and the cellar would still be there, the two of us dug down in the bottom corner.

Everything in the dining room trembled as we passed through again. Shadow and light mixed in a frightening dance on the other side of the lace curtains. The winds began to take on a human sound, a moan under the hiss and growl of air. I opened the back door and the handle jerked out of my grip before the door slammed into the outside wall. The sky was full of topsoil and leaves, twigs, even a gardening glove with fingers flapping.

I didn't know I had only a handful of minutes. Or that the cellar was a mistake. That strange feeling in my gut, that something wonderful might be just around the corner, flared back up inside me as we stepped out the kitchen door and into the wind. A thrill shot through me. God made the storm just as God made the rainbow and the calm that comes after the storm. God made the earth and all that dwelled there and also heaven and hell and all the angels and devils that dwell there, too. So there is God in everything, in the wind and the rain and the burning white of lightning.

Maybe if I could have held on to that thought, I might have left that cellar for heaven instead of hell. But then, I never would have found James. So maybe God truly was in the rising water and the darkness and the terror. His eye, the unblinking funnel of cloud at the center of my panic.

CHAPTER 8

Helen

T HE SOUND OF A DOORBELL still hung in the air. I watched Jenny,
how her eyes darted back and forth — she listened to the sound of
footsteps and muffled voices in the hall.

"Jenny?" It was Cathy's voice, Jenny's mother, just outside the
bathroom door. "Are you feeling sick?" The handle turned, but the
door stayed shut.

Jenny twisted the faucet until the water shut off. Next a male
voice was on the other side of the door — I knew who it was because I had already witnessed this scene.

"Jenny? Can I talk to you?"

It wasn't James, of course, simply the body he had borrowed, but
the sound still thrilled me.

"Honey, there's someone here to see you," called Cathy.

Jenny opened her mouth to speak, but her chin was quivering.

"I'm serious." Cathy's tone was harsh. "This is your mother
speaking. You let me in this minute." She was making the hinges
rattle.

"Are you hurt?" His voice again.

Jenny finally answered. "No." But too soft to be heard.

"Open this door!" Cathy's tone was high-pitched now, on the brink of panic. "I'm going to call the police." The door shook so hard, the empty pill bottle on the floor bounced. "I'm calling 911!"

"I'm all right!" Jenny shouted. Then she looked at me, but of course she couldn't see me. At least I didn't think she could.

Although I knew it was going to happen, I still jumped when the door burst in, cracking the wood frame, and Billy Blake crashed into the room like a fireman.

Jenny blinked at him. She held her knees up to her chest, hiding her nakedness.

"Are you okay?" he asked. He was breathing hard as if he'd run for miles to get to her. I was not in love with Billy, of course, but that particular shade of brown hair and the shape of those hands made my heart ache.

"I don't know," said Jenny.

He tore a bath towel off the rack and bent down on one knee, unfolding it over her shoulders like a cape.

"I'm sorry I said I didn't remember you," he told her, "when you came to see me today."

"I came to see you?"

So, she didn't remember what her body had done while I was its captain. I was not surprised.

Billy reached to the back pocket of his jeans. "After you left, I found this in my room."

He held the shiny plastic square in front of Jenny, a photo. "This is us," he said.

Jenny brought the picture closer to her face, tilting it so that the glare on the glossy finish shifted. I knew that picture, of course. To

Jenny the photo would look like a picture of her and Billy, but it was actually James and me while we occupied their bodies—it was the only way for us to be together.

A drop of water from Jenny's hand ran down the white border.

"I'm having some trouble remembering things," Billy told her.

"Me too," she said.

"You look happy with me," he said, as if astonished that someone could ever love him.

Jenny looked pleased, but she was still dazed. "Yeah, I do," she told him. He started to rub the towel on her head, drying her cold hair. "Is your name Billy?" she asked.

"Yeah."

Here was all I remembered seeing before I left earth.

Cathy, the phone to her ear, stopped in the bathroom doorway. "Jennifer!"

It was strange to think that I had left this bathroom and climbed to heaven, into James's arms. That was happening at the same time that I was standing here and looking down at Jenny. I could not regret now that I had become a ghost, because how else would I have met James? Yet looking back, my inability to cross into heaven for so many years seemed foolish.

Cathy snapped her fingers at Jenny. "Cover yourself!" Then she motioned for Billy to get out. "Do you mind?"

Billy backed into the hall as Cathy closed the door in his face. "Why don't they answer?" Cathy scowled at the phone, pressed two buttons, listened again. "How many did you take?" she asked.

Jenny searched the room as if she felt watched.

"How many?" Cathy demanded.

"I'm not overdosing," said Jenny. "I threw them up."

"Were you trying to kill yourself?"

"No." Jenny paused. I could tell she didn't remember one way or the other. "I spilled them and the ones I swallowed I threw up. Don't call an ambulance."

Cathy tried to dress her daughter as if the girl were five years old — buttoned her buttons, flicked her collar down straight, pulled her hair out of her sweater for her.

Cathy agreed to drive Jenny to the emergency room instead of calling the paramedics. When they emerged from the bathroom at last, Cathy shooed Billy out of the house, rushing to gather her purse and keys.

She bustled Jenny through the kitchen toward the door that led into the garage, but Jenny was staring at the house — the broken picture frames in the living room and dining room, the mess in the kitchen as if someone had pulled half the contents of the cupboards out and dumped them onto the floor and into the sink.

I floated after them the way I used to follow my hosts everywhere. Before I met James I'd had a chain of five humans I'd haunted since my death. I found safety from my hell by clinging to them and did what I could to be a friend to each. But Jenny was the only one of the Quick I had ever possessed.

I sat in the back seat behind her as the engine roared. Cathy couldn't wait for the garage door to rise — the car's antenna snapped off and clattered onto the driveway.

Billy was waiting on the sidewalk. Cathy slammed on the brakes and rolled down her window. "Go home," she ordered him.

Jenny leaned forward, about to speak, when she saw Mitch.

Wearing a grease-stained T-shirt, Billy's brother stood leaning against his wreck of a car parked at the curb. Cathy's angry tone drew his attention. He threw his lit cigarette onto the lawn.

"Is she okay?" Billy asked Cathy.

"If you don't leave I'll have to call the police," Cathy told him.

"Mom!"

Mitch strode toward them.

Cathy rammed the car into park and got out, taking a step toward Mitch before he could get any closer.

"Will you please take your son home?" asked Cathy. She took in his appearance: unshaven face, muscled arms, tattoos. She held her sweater closed as if he could see through her garments.

"He's not my kid, he's my brother." Mitch gave her a sweeping glance, head to foot.

Cathy bristled. "Where are your parents while all this is happening?"

Mitch smiled. "Who the hell do you think you are?"

Billy stood with his hands in his pockets now, watching Jenny through the car window, seemingly oblivious to the argument. And Jenny stared back at him, but she jumped at the sound of angry voices. I didn't want her to worry.

"All will be well," I told her, but she couldn't hear me with so many distractions.

When I left heaven I had a clear plan as to how I would help Jenny. In the same way that I had guided my hosts with an invisible touch on the arm, keeping them from stumbling on an unnoticed stone in their path, I planned to lay my hand on Jenny's shoulder when she was faced with Billy Blake and turn her from him. After all, it was James and I who had been in love, not Billy and Jenny. She should feel no obligation.

When Jenny's mother treated her with harshness I imagined I would sit between them, holding each by the hand, and act as the conduit for love as I had with my Poet and his dying brother. And if Jenny's father were to reappear and throw hurtful words, I would stand like a shield in his face and dampen his wickedness as I had when my Knight was confronted by an angry colleague. And if Jenny found the consequences of my time in her life kept her from sleep, I would sit on the foot of her bed and sing to her, or recite verse, as I did when banishing the nightmares of my Playwright.

But what I had forgotten was that those moments with my hosts were the exceptions. It was a rare thing to affect the realm of the Quick.

Cathy's voice quavered. "Well, tell your mother for me that it's impossible for your brother and my daughter to continue seeing each other."

"Tell her yourself. She's at St. Jude's Hospital, but she hasn't said a word in five years." Mitch enjoyed her surprise. "Or, my dad's in the county prison. Or you could mind your damn business."

Cathy took a flustered step backwards, bumping into the car. "Watch your language in front of my child."

"Fuck you, lady." Mitch grabbed Billy by the sleeve and pulled him toward their car.

Cathy hurried back into the driver's seat, white in the face. The car accelerated, then left the driveway at an odd angle, scouring the tailpipe on the curb.

"Billy wants to help," said Jenny. "He tried to save me."

Cathy was breathing too fast. She sat with her shoulders high and tight. She should have at least tried to put on a calm front for her daughter's sake. But Cathy offered not one word of reassurance. I had planned to draw them closer, and I could have sat between them now and taken their hands, but I didn't want to touch Cathy. It angered me that she offered Jenny no sympathy. I didn't want to try to make Cathy a better mother. I wanted to comfort Jenny myself. Someone had to protect the girl.

Even though she might not hear, I leaned forward and whispered to the back of Jenny's head of gold hair, "Don't worry. Everything will be all right."

"Why wouldn't you open the door?" Cathy asked her.

"The door?" said Jenny. "You mean the bathroom door?"

"Yes, the bathroom door!" Cathy, who hadn't fastened her safety belt, now tried to force the strap over her chest, but it had locked in place.

"I don't know." Jenny peered into the back seat, looking through me. "Maybe I didn't want to get out of the tub." Then she asked, "Who else was at the house?"

"What?" Cathy glanced at her. "You mean Billy's brother?"

"No," said Jenny. "Wasn't there someone else in the bathroom?"

CHAPTER 9

Helen

WHAT ARE YOU TALKING ABOUT?" said Cathy.

A queer tremor rippled through me. *I* was the someone who had been in the bathroom with them, standing beside the tub.

"Other than that boy?" Cathy asked.

Jenny caught sight of something outside the car—she pivoted in her seat. I wondered what had captured her attention. We passed store window displays filled with autumn leaves and the silhouettes of crows.

"Why are there pumpkins everywhere?" she asked.

I didn't know exactly how long Jenny had been away from her body before I entered it, but I knew it must be unsettling to be thrown blindly back into her life. If she could have seen me, I would have smiled at her, because her mother's expression was far from soothing.

"What is wrong with you?" Cathy demanded. "How many pills did you really take?"

Jenny stared at her mother as if something was missing—I could see it in her blue eyes and feel it in the trembling of her narrow shoulders. She was afraid.

"Mom?" Jenny asked. "Where's Daddy?"

Cathy started weeping as she drove. "He's probably at *her* house."

"Whose house?"

But Cathy wouldn't answer. She muttered to herself and strangled the steering wheel with twisting fists. She drove past a stop sign without slowing down and did not seem even to hear the honking horns. This danger she was exposing her child to made me wish I could take over Cathy's body the way I had Jenny's.

I had been an imperfect protector for my own daughter, but I knew I could be a better mother to Jenny than Cathy was proving to be. It struck me then that even if I hadn't been able to save myself, I could have acted as a kind of guardian angel to my daughter as she grew up if I'd been clever enough to find my way into heaven sooner. Instead, I was foolish and frightened and got stuck. I'd been taught by my father how to milk a cow and at my mother's side how to make shortbread. But no one had taught me how to die.

❦

At the emergency room, we were escorted into a cubicle, where Jenny sat staring at her hands. I stood behind her chair. The small space flickered with fairylike lights from the fluorescent overheads and reflected off Cathy's diamond wedding ring as she furiously filled out a form on a clipboard.

I wanted to point out how pretty the twinkling lights were, but Jenny couldn't hear me, of course, and she wasn't a baby. She was a grown girl.

The nurse asked many questions and Cathy answered them, never making eye contact with her daughter. Jenny could probably have stood up and walked away and her mother would not have noticed. I took a seat in the empty plastic chair to Jenny's right.

"The nurse is asking you a question." Cathy tapped on Jenny's knee as if the girl had been napping in church.

"So, you threw up the sleeping pills," asked the nurse. "Is that right?"

"That's right," she said.

"But she's having memory problems," Cathy insisted.

The nurse asked Jenny about alcohol, drugs, head injuries. She took Jenny's pulse, blood pressure, temperature. All the while I thought of the things I would want to hear if I were Jenny: *Don't worry about a thing—we'll take care of you.*

Finally we were taken into the emergency room examination area. The doctor was reading his clipboard when he pulled open the curtain. He wheeled a little stool up to the narrow bed where Jenny sat on a white paper sheet. He sat down, smiled, a neutral expression.

"You're having trouble with your memory." He clicked his pen. "What did you have for breakfast?"

"I don't remember," she said.

"Do you know today's date?" he asked.

"No." Jenny looked embarrassed. "Is it fall? It doesn't feel like fall to me."

"That so?" The doctor scribbled a note. "Why?"

Jenny flexed her hands, felt her face as if she was still getting used to being back inside her own flesh. "Not sure," she said.

"What were you doing before you came here?" he asked.

"Taking a bath," said Jenny.

"And before that?" The doctor, whose tag read DR. A. LAWRENCE, waited, his eyebrows raised.

"I wish I knew," Jenny admitted.

"What's the last thing you remember before the bath?"

Jenny swallowed uncomfortably. She slipped her hands under her thighs and stared at her knees for a moment. "I remember being in the Prayer Corner."

"That wasn't this morning," Cathy said. "We didn't have Bible study today."

"How long ago was that, the morning you're thinking of?" the doctor asked Jenny. "Any idea?"

She sighed. I sensed her mind spinning with images, though I could not see the story of pictures there. "I remember going on a trip . . ." Jenny's voice trailed away.

"Speak up, Jennifer," Cathy ordered.

I lay my hand on Jenny's arm and the familiar tingle of spirit touching the living licked through me, cold and warm at the same time.

I did not sense in Jenny any recognition that I had tried to comfort her by my touch. She was still shaking and pale. But I was sure she would learn to recognize my help.

Claims made by the Quick as to the powers of ghosts are often exaggerated. It was difficult for me to move any object in the world of the living. Emotions are what can be heard or at least sensed by the living, rarely one's voice—sometimes the touch of my hand, but more often it was my desire to reach out.

"I think I went to the country," said Jenny. "There was a field—"

"No." Cathy shook her head. "We haven't taken a trip since last summer, and it was to Sacramento."

If Jenny remembered anything more, she didn't speak it aloud. But she did look at my hand where it lay on her arm. She lifted her own hand slowly as I drew mine away. She rubbed the place where I had touched her. Then she flexed her fingers and looked around, her gaze passing through me.

She may not have realized it was me beside her, but I had at least changed something in her world. It was a start.

The doctor must have noticed that Jenny was shaking—he took a folded blanket from the foot of the examination table and handed it to her. "Did you have a recent upset?"

Jenny took the blanket absently.

"Anything frighten you or make you sad?" he asked. "Did you have a fight with someone?"

Cathy took the blanket from Jenny's hands and snapped it open, then put it around her daughter's shoulders as she spoke. "She hasn't been herself for days now." Cathy sat back down and watched the doctor's pen as if wanting to dictate what he recorded. "She started seeing a boy in secret." Her voice dropped. "Intimately."

Jenny pulled the blanket around her as if trying to hide a scarlet letter her mother had sewn onto her blouse.

Cathy looked humiliated to add what followed, "And her father left." She folded her hands and held them down in her lap. "He moved out this morning. Jenny found out about it right before her bath."

This was no surprise to me—I'd still been Jenny then. Cathy had wept with me about her husband, Dan, running off with another woman and then we'd celebrated by burning down the Prayer Corner. But Jenny's head came up, her eyes wide.

"Do you remember hearing about that?" the doctor asked her, and Jenny shook her head no.

"How does it make you feel?" he asked.

I was afraid Jenny would be hurt—he was, after all, her father. I would have been devastated if my own Papa had left me when I was a girl.

"Confused," said Jenny.

"That's understandable," the doctor told her.

The questions were over for a while, but there were hours of waiting—they performed many tests. There were machines for tracking brain waves, diagramming the inside of the head, making a graph of heart patterns—little tubes of blood were taken from Jenny's arm. They taped a ball of cotton to the tiny wound and Cathy brought the girl a bottle of orange juice and a muffin. This should have been a sweet gesture, but in the same way Cathy had flicked the hospital blanket around Jenny's shoulders without asking her if she was cold or frightened, Cathy applied food and drink as if Jenny were a dish that needed drying or a dress that needed mending.

The way the nurses, wearing matching pale blue uniforms, busied themselves around Jenny's body, measuring blood and checking monitors and applying disinfectant, reminded me of cooks preparing a feast. Jenny, watching them, looked as anxious as the Christmas goose about to be cooked.

Cathy looked nervous, as well, but didn't include herself in the scene. Couldn't the woman see that Jenny needed to be held and comforted? I ached with the realization that I had never been able to take my own girl in my arms when she was Jenny's age. Not one afternoon spent together when she was old enough to tell me her dreams. It was torture to observe Cathy sitting blindly and stupidly beside her daughter when I would have given anything just to brush my daughter's hair one single night when she was fifteen.

⌐

Even though every test showed that Jenny was healthy, I knew she was not all right. I'd made a plan to help her, but this rescue was not an easy thing.

"Where are we going?" Jenny asked her mother.

I had little experience with the order of these streets, but even I could tell that Cathy was not driving us home. And she wouldn't explain. Jenny watched her with concern.

Eventually we stopped in front a tiny house with a porch swing outside the front window.

"Mom," Jenny said. "Why are we at Mrs. Morgan's house?"

There were two cars, tail to nose, in the narrow driveway. One was a white van.

"Why is Dad's car here?" Jenny asked.

Cathy let the engine idle in the middle of the street for a moment, staring at the lights shining through the curtained windows, then she dug the heel of her hand into the steering wheel, blaring the horn in a savage blast before pulling away.

"Daddy left us for Mrs. Morgan?" Jenny shook her mother's arm, but Cathy wouldn't look at her or answer. "Isn't she your prayer partner?"

Cathy wept, silently steering with one hand, the other pressed to her middle as if she might be sick.

As the car neared Jenny's driveway, I saw a piece of white paper sticking out of their front door. Cathy pulled into the garage, but as soon as she entered the house, she walked straight to the front door from inside, opened it, and pulled out the note.

"Is that for me?" asked Jenny.

Cathy slammed the door and locked it. "No." She unfolded the page and gave it a quick glance. I saw, before she crumpled it, that it was a phone number and looked like Billy's handwriting. "It's nothing."

Jenny followed her mother into the kitchen and watched her toss the ball of paper into the sink. I think Jenny might have protested but the mess in the kitchen distracted her.

The sink was splattered with an odd mix of foods. Vegetable drinks, protein powder, and granola. Perhaps Dan's favorites. The jars and cans still lay open around the drain. The tall rubbish can nearby overflowed with half-empty packages of molasses cookies, seaweed crackers, and power bars. A nearly full jar of fig jam was crammed in the top, upside down, where I assumed Cathy had stuffed it after Dan walked out.

"I didn't do this, did I?" asked Jenny

When her mother failed to answer, Jenny followed her down the hall.

The dining room and living room were littered with broken

glass and bent picture frames. Photos of Jenny's family had been mutilated so that her father's image was torn or twisted from each picture. The only one still on the wall was of Jenny as a baby, alone beside a little wading pool.

Cathy kept walking, down the hall and into the office, where many shelves had been emptied. A pile of books — business advice, sports memoirs, and how-to manuals. Two tan rectangles of un-faded paint were left under empty nails on the wall where Dan's diplomas used to hang.

Cathy stepped around the piles and sat at the desk. She picked up the phone and stared at it for a moment before she began to push numbered buttons — not a word to her daughter. Jenny paused for a moment, took in the new imbalance in what had been a very tidy room.

"Bev?" Cathy said, her voice quavering. "Something's hap-pened."

Jenny continued down the hall and into the family room, and I followed, wanting to tell her what had happened that day.

The smoke alarm cover dangled at the top of the doorway; a liquor decanter lay empty on the carpet. The floor was strewn with board games, pink and blue paper money, dice, Scrabble tiles. And there in the far corner, where Jenny used to sit with her parents every morning for Bible study and prayers, where I had to sit with them just yesterday (if that was possible), there the three chairs lay broken and charred atop a huge melted burn mark in the rug. The Bible itself I had saved — it sat on the arm of the sofa — but Jenny saw another book had been torn to shreds and singed. Scraps of burnt pages and the twisted brown binding lay all around the chairs. Could she tell it was her journal? Jenny picked up what was left of the diary she was once forced to keep. The pages were mostly gone. A jagged wing of paper fluttered from the spine as she dropped it back into the ashes.

She looked up—a black cloud hung above this mess, a smoke stain, four feet wide, on the ceiling.

"Jenny." I spoke her name and she turned, but not to me. She looked at the doorway and her mother appeared, eyes red, arms filled with cleaning supplies.

"We made the mess together, we'll clean it up together," said Cathy.

Jenny looked proud. "We did this together?"

Cathy handed her a scrub brush and a spray can of spot remover. "We need to make it right before anyone sees it," she said, pulling on a pair of yellow rubber gloves and kneeling in the Prayer Corner.

CHAPTER 10

Helen

His cheeks were pinked from the wind and his hair ruffled. A strand stuck to his forehead in a curl that made my heart ache.

"Hey." He smiled, hands in his pockets.

"Hey." Jenny moved back, swinging the door wide, and he stepped in.

She had rescued his note from the kitchen sink, where her mother had thrown it, unfolded the page that was covered in running ink, and managed to read his phone number. She called him in secret that night. She told him what time Cathy was planning to meet a friend's divorce lawyer the next morning. It was understandable that Jenny and Billy wanted to be alone—they may not remember becoming a couple, but they were bound by the union all the same. I had planned on guiding Jenny away from this entanglement, but I couldn't help having a fondness for Billy even though he was not James. If I didn't keep them apart, I wasn't sure he would make Jenny happy for long.

After glancing to see if anyone outside had seen Billy arrive, Jenny closed the door. Perhaps Billy had walked. Mitch didn't drop him off and the rusty car was not parked outside.

Billy took his hands from his pockets, but didn't know whether to embrace her. Jenny was blushing.

"I don't really remember you," she told him. "I mean, I know who you are from school."

"Me too." He shrugged. "It's weird."

Not as simple as it looked, this meeting, for most young men and women who begin a courtship do not have a forgotten history between them. They seemed like such children. Her hands were smooth, with rounded fingertips like a little girl's.

"Are you sure that's me in that picture?" Jenny asked him. They stood in the foyer.

"I wondered that too," said Billy. "Why would a girl like you go out with someone like me? But Mitch says it's you."

"I didn't mean it that way." Jenny reached out to touch his arm but never quite got there.

He shrugged. "Okay."

"Want to see the house?" she asked. "I mean, the rest of the house. You probably remember my bathroom."

This made him smile.

Jenny and Billy were dressed like opposites, from two sides of the chess board. He wore faded black pants and a dark gray sweatshirt turned wrong side out. She wore light cotton pants rolled up at the ankles and a long white shirt. They were lovely, awkward creatures.

She led him into the kitchen and I followed at a respectable distance.

"It's really . . . clean," he said.

Each room reminded me of another problem I had caused: the dining room table where I had pretended to do Jenny's homework — I had been a shameful student and completely abandoned her studies for a week; in the living room nearly a dozen family photographs had been taken down, which reminded me that I had taken photographs with Jenny's camera without permission — she had gone to a great deal of trouble to keep her picture-taking a secret. It was sacred territory, and I should not have trespassed.

Billy stopped by the living room sofa, stared at the carpet, the ceiling, in wonder. "It's huge. You could set up a skateboard pit in here." Then he homed in on the one unsmashed frame left on the wall. It held a picture of Jenny taken at perhaps one year old. The baby girl was standing beside a rubber wading pool, holding a beach ball, wearing a one-piece daisy bathing suit bulging with built-in lifejacket floats. Her wet hair made her appear nearly bald, and her tiny round ears stuck out like handles. The camera had caught her in a giddy laugh.

I knew exactly what she felt like on that afternoon fourteen years before, though that was impossible, of course. Yet I remembered the squirmy weight of her and the cool damp skin with the warmth of her underneath. The smell of her wet hair. The sound of her smacking lips as she teethed on her own fingers. The way she kept turning her head while I tried to comb her tangled hair.

You're wrong, I told myself. *You're thinking of your own baby.* Perhaps coming back from heaven had rattled my mind — my memories were pieces of two puzzles mixed together.

Billy came up close to the photo, tapped the frame with one finger. "Look at you, you little monkey."

In the hall there was a Bible quote from Colossians in cross-stitching framed under glass: *Live a life worthy of the Lord.*

I was reminded of another of my sins — I had not only ranted at the women in Cathy's church group (an episode I suspected would stain her reputation in that congregation), but also raged at Cathy, said hurtful and peculiar things—I actually told her that I was not her daughter. But since I was wearing her daughter's body, she didn't believe me.

As Jenny led Billy farther down the hall, he paused at the bathroom door and fingered the latch that he had broken the day before. "Sorry," he told her.

Jenny blushed again, I suppose not knowing what to say.

Which brought me to a more serious sin—I had taken Jenny's deflowering away from her and exposed her to Billy's body unprotected. I had no idea how foolish the boy had been in his short past, and neither had James. It was thoughtless and selfish of me to have changed Jenny's reputation at school, linking her not only with Billy but with my beloved Mr. Brown. That false gossip about an English teacher having taken advantage of a student was buzzing about the high school, and probably the whole community, was appalling. I told Jenny's parents that it was James—well, Billy—who was my lover and not Mr. Brown, and I think they believed me, but the harm had already been done.

"What happened here?" Billy asked when they got to the family room. The Prayer Corner had been neatened, the burn on the carpet hidden with a throw rug. But the charred ceiling looked like the mouth of hell.

"Sort of a protest thing when my father left."

"You never said you were a pyromaniac."

When Jenny opened the door to the master bedroom neither crossed the threshold. "My mother's room," she told him.

He peered in with no comment. Next the office, where several boxes of Dan's belongings cluttered the middle of the floor, awaiting their fate.

"It's kind of messy in here," said Jenny.

Billy gave a little laugh. "You should see our place." Then he caught her eye. "I guess you've already seen it."

"I don't remember that," said Jenny.

"Believe me, you're not missing anything."

I didn't expect Jenny to know what had happened while she was away from her body, yet I had secretly hoped I had left some residual haunting, some scent or hue that would give her a sense of me. But she seemed completely unaware of me or James.

Billy squeezed past her into the office and tilted his head as he read the titles of books left on the shelves. *The Christian Wife, The Bible Diet, A Mother/Daughter Walk with God.* "Man, your family is religious. No offense."

"It's okay." She tried to sound lighthearted, but her sigh was weighty.

Finally she led him into her own bedroom and he followed without hesitation. Jenny sat on the bed and watched him study everything in sight: the girlish white dressing table, the orderly closet where the sliding mirrored doors were left half open, the view from the window into the pristine garden. He stopped at the painting of the praying hands.

"How did we get together?" He said it as if it was a rhetorical question.

Jenny didn't answer him, but instead asked, "What's the last thing you remember before your memory gap?"

"I was at a park near my house," he said. "Getting high."

"So you had a drug blackout?"

"I guess. I was just trying everything that day. Whatever I could get my hands on. Pot, pills, Super Glue."

"That's awful," said Jenny.

But if he hadn't, I thought, *I never would have met James.*

"Yeah. That was maybe two or three weeks ago." Billy leaned on the wall beside her desk like a loiterer. I admired him for not sitting on the bed beside her. "So what kind of amnesia do you have?"

"Unexplained." Then she frowned. "Do you think we could have done drugs together?"

"Jeez, I hope not." Billy looked ill for a moment.

I wanted to tell them the story James had told me about his taking over Billy's body, but I was left out of the conversation.

"No, that can't be it," said Jenny. "My missing time is months long, not weeks."

"When did you wake up?" he asked her. "I mean, when did your blackout stop?"

"Yesterday."

"Shit," Billy whispered. "Day before yesterday."

Now both of them looked unnerved. He pulled out the desk chair and sat.

"That's really weird," said Jenny.

"When I came out of it, I was visiting my dad in prison. Mitch was just unloading on him. Having this massive meltdown. I guess that was what woke me up." Billy shrugged as if apologizing for knowing so little about his own life.

I ached at the core remembering the last time I saw James in Billy's body, disappearing down the hall at the prison with Mitch. I missed James so badly that the floor creaked under me, but neither of the other two noticed.

"Turns out, right before I woke up, my mother told me my father was moving out," said Jenny.

"That sucks," said Billy. "Or not. If it was my dad we would've had a party." He waved his hand in front of her then, as if erasing the last remark. "Sorry. Rewind that."

"Do you think shock can bring you back from amnesia?" asked Jenny.

"Sure. I guess." He studied her for a moment, not just her eyes. "It's hard coming back."

"Yeah."

"Yesterday afternoon I felt like I was on the wrong planet." He thought for a second, seeming haunted, then laughed it off. "I lay in the grass out in our backyard like an idiot, just staring at the sky."

CHAPTER 11

Helen

SOME SORROW OR FEAR FLICKERED behind Billy's eyes again, but he reined it in. "I felt like one of those animals that wakes up in the zoo after the tranquilizer dart wears off. 'Hey, man, where's my jungle?'" Billy used a comical voice for the animal, then looked embarrassed. "I mean, I wanted to come back and see Mitch again, but I felt like I'd left something behind somewhere else."

"You did lose something," Jenny said. "You lost time."

"Yeah. Missing time and my memory," said Billy. "Like, I don't remember what I said or did that made you like me."

Jenny's cheeks and throat burned pink. Billy wasn't James, but he had his own charm.

"Bet you don't either," he said. "I get the feeling if you got a do-over you wouldn't hook up with me again."

"Why do you say that?" Jenny asked.

His expression was not unkind. "Maybe I was less geeky during my blackout, and maybe you were temporarily insane while you had amnesia, but girls like you don't even start conversations with me."

Billy would have been shocked to know how appealing James

had been in his "Billy" disguise and how mad I truly had been to be with him in my "Jenny" mask.

"Are you saying I'm stuck-up?" Jenny folded her arms at him, looking a little like Cathy. "If you can't remember me, how would you know what I'm like?"

"I said I don't remember hooking up with you," he pointed out. "I didn't say I didn't remember you. I've been going to the same school as you since fourth grade."

Jenny dropped her defenses. She tucked her legs up under her on the edge of the bed. "We were never in the same class in elementary school."

"We had the same recess sometimes," he said. "We took the same bus for a while."

"Okay," she said. "You knew I existed. But you didn't really notice me."

"I did so, but it's not like I could just walk up to you and start cracking jokes." When she looked unconvinced, Billy said, "You don't believe I knew who you were? You sat in the front on the left in Mr. Fancher's class."

I could see that he was right. Jenny looked startled.

"One day during lunch when they were showing a movie in the library on one of those crappy old TVs, you were walking past the building and you stopped and watched through the window. It was some ballet thing."

"*The Red Shoes.*" Jenny looked curious now. "Where were you?"

"Detention, in a folding chair outside the principal's office."

She smiled.

Billy looked determined now to prove her wrong, and it touched me that he had gathered and held so many memories of her.

"One day in the hall in seventh grade," he told her, "you looked really sad and you dropped your math book and I almost reached down and got it for you, because you took so long to pick it up yourself, but my friends were with me."

"You must've noticed lots of girls," said Jenny.

"You were different," he said. "You were mysterious."

"Yeah, right."

"I caught you in your lunchtime Bible club, or whatever it's called, looking at the sky when everyone else had their heads down and their eyes closed. I wondered what you were seeing that they couldn't see," said Billy.

Jenny rubbed her arms as if she was chilled. I felt then like an intruder. But I was compelled to listen to this unfolding of their childhoods.

"I knew you," Billy told Jenny. "*You're* the one who never noticed *me*."

"I did," she protested. "I remembered your name, didn't I?"

"You know, you don't have to say hi to me at school, if you don't want to."

Jenny sat up straight. "What are you talking about?"

"At school people might think we're going out, but it's kind of like we're just meeting for the first time here, so don't feel like you have to stay friends with me." Billy held up his hands as if to say there were no strings attached. "Everyone will just assume you dumped me."

"Do you want to break up?" she asked.

He squinted at her, perhaps trying to discern her mood. "Are we still going out?"

To his apparent surprise, Jenny started laughing.

"It's not funny," he said, but he was smiling.

"No, it's really sort of creepy and confusing." She sighed. "Sorry. It's just nerves."

"I suck at talking to girls," said Billy.

I had lived with Mr. Brown as my host for years, which included innumerable college parties, but I couldn't help wishing Billy spoke with James's vocabulary.

"Except for you," said Billy. "So I'd be okay with you giving me a chance," he said.

"Is that because I'm not like a real girl to you?" she asked. "Am I too much like a sister?"

"Ummm." He chose his words carefully. "I've never had a sister, so it's not like I have a lot of experience with this, but when I'm around you, I don't think you could call what I'm feeling brotherly."

I started pacing between them. Something worried me about this conversation. I had the queerest wrestling of emotions about Billy Blake. Part of me was not sure he was worthy of her, but I was willing to give him a chance. I wanted to test him — send him on a quest like a knight courting a princess. If he really wanted her, he should fight for her. Come back with a dragon's head.

"I think I remember something you did in junior high," Jenny told him. She was looking into his eyes, but also through him into the past perhaps. "At the Cinco de Mayo fair, when I was in seventh grade, I was standing in line to enter this contest and my mom left me alone while she went to buy tickets for the booths. I'd made this model of a Spanish mission out of clay that I was really proud of. There were these three boys standing nearby and one of them said my mission looked like barfed-up gum and another one of them said no it doesn't and to leave her alone and then all three started having a fight and knocked over a display."

"Actually it was a bake sale table."

"See?" She laughed. "I remembered you."

I stopped pacing and looked at Billy. *Well done, Mr. Blake*, I told him.

"Barfed-up gum?" Billy shook his head. "What a dick."

I bristled at this.

"I know!" said Jenny.

"I should have kicked his ass."

"Didn't you?"

"Well, it was two against one," said Billy. "I was outnumbered."

Good lad, I told him. Language aside, his actions were gallant.

"Why did you hang around with them?" she asked him.

He shrugged. "They let me. I was kind of a loner. I didn't have real friends after sixth grade."

"I never had close friends either."

"What about that crowd of church girls?"

For a moment Jenny looked tired and thin, with shadowed eyes, but it was just the lighting in the room. A flame lantern would help. And lace curtains. Her room lacked warmth. If I were her mother I would put a quilt on her bed instead of that bloodless white blanket. I knew exactly which one—the blue and green honeycomb pattern. It had snatches of my daughter's first dresses, the navy gingham and the green stripes, and squares made from my own girlhood clothes, blue roses and a brown plaid faded to bone.

And she needed books in this room, of course. Now that I was here I would surround her with them, stand them up proudly on every surface.

And I wasn't using my dresses anymore. I would hold them up under her hair and choose the one that suited her eyes best. I would pick out the old dry thread and sew them afresh. I would rub lemon juice into the stains on the lace. I would take up the hems for her. Only an inch, for we were so alike, she and I.

I found I was sitting on the bed now, behind Jenny, holding up my hands between the seams of her sleeves with a measuring tape that did not exist. When I realized that I'd forgotten we were a world apart, I withered back from her, ashamed that I had become so muddled.

Billy's voice rattled me out of my daze.

"Maybe we're not that different," he was saying. "That'd be freaky."

"Were you lonely too?" Jenny asked him.

He looked uncomfortable. Maybe this wasn't something young men admitted.

"Well, here we are, keeping each other company," said Jenny.

"Yeah," he said. "Some things you just can't do alone."

"Like have a conversation," she said.

"Or tell knock-knock jokes."

"Do you want to tell me a knock-knock joke?" asked Jenny.

"I'm good for now." Absently he tilted the chair back on two legs. "What have you always wanted to do but couldn't do without a friend?"

Jenny blinked, her shoulders shifted a little. That was all, but both Billy and I could see that she was thinking of something that she did not speak aloud.

"You thought of something," he said. "What is it?"

"Nothing," she insisted.

"Come on," he coaxed her. "What could be weirder than what we've already been through?"

"There's things I could never do in ballet because you have to have a partner."

"I could help," said Billy.

I moved to the corner of the room and began to seep into the wall — I was invading their privacy.

"I don't dance anymore," said Jenny. "I quit taking ballet in March."

"How come?"

"I needed more time to study." Jenny thought for a moment. "My father thought so, anyway."

"Bastard."

Jenny couldn't slap a hand over her mouth before the laugh got away from her.

"Sorry," said Billy, but he looked pleased. "You were the one who had an indoor bonfire party when he left."

"It's okay." Jenny folded her hands shyly.

"So let's do it." He let the chair drop to four legs. "You have a partner now."

"Really? You dance ballet?"

"I've seen those guys on TV." Billy stood up and put a foot on the seat of the chair, motioned dramatically to the right. "They just stand there and go *Here she is!*" He turned to the left as if displaying a piece of art. "And *Look at her now,* and"—he mimicked catching an invisible bag of flour—"*Oops, I better catch her because she just threw herself at me.*"

Jenny laughed and I blessed him for that. It was a sweet sound. "You do *not* want to dance with me," said Jenny.

"Oh yeah?" The mischief in his eyes reminded me of James. He pushed the chair out of the way with his foot. "Go get your tutu."

Jenny took her box of ballet things off the closet shelf and opened it slowly, drawing the toe shoes up by their ribbons.

He watched her sit on the side of the bed and lace them up her ankles, the wide satin ribbons faded and frayed in places, the toes of the shoes fuzzy and nearly worn to the wood. She stood up, hopped onto toe, paused to flex her calves and shake out her knees. Still he watched her. He seemed to have become hypnotized, but a moment later he stepped up to her side as Jenny approached the mirrored closet doors.

"This is silly," she said. "You don't have to do this."

"You calling me a quitter?"

"No music in my room anymore," she said. "Sorry."

"Bastard," he repeated in a whisper, and Jenny smiled, but I could see the truth in it made her a little uneasy. She shifted into position with her feet together and her posture lifted as she spread her arms. She elongated herself, through her spine and limbs—a remembered strength hidden there opened like a blossom. She began to quietly sing a simple melody, perhaps a favorite ballet theme.

"And she sings, too," Billy muttered.

"Stop it," she laughed, and looked into his eyes in the reflection.

I would have been in the reflected scene, in the wall behind them, if I had been one of the living.

The energy wavered in Jenny's arms and she stopped singing. Something in the reflection had startled her. She dropped from her toes to stand flat-footed. Something in the backwards picture of Billy's face made her stare.

PART 3

CHAPTER 12

Jenny

He CRACKED HIS KNUCKLES AND shook out his shoulders like a boxer ready for the first round. My feelings about Billy kept shifting. At first it seemed like a dream, how he broke down the bathroom door to rescue me. But every time I thought about that picture he'd showed me, with our naked shoulders in bed, and about how we'd made love and I didn't even remember it, my stomach jumped like an electric eel. On the other hand, it was exciting that I had found his phone number and called him behind my mother's back. Then I was nervous when he first showed up—I acted like an idiot. Finally I started to feel comfortable with him. I'd never liked a boy who liked me back.

But when I looked at him in the mirror, I had the feeling I was supposed to be somewhere else and with someone else. Maybe it was everything that had happened the day before, crashing in on me. Having lost my memory and going to the hospital. Finding out my father left us. Finding out that Billy and I had been together—that was unbelievable, that I'd missed having my first boyfriend. My head felt light and fuzzy.

I stared at Billy in the mirror—there I was, standing right next to him, but it was like I'd gotten off a bus at the wrong stop.

I knew mirrors lied. You always see yourself in a reflection, so you're used to it. But when you see the face of someone you know in a mirror, it looks backwards. Did I know Billy well enough to think he looked wrong?

"Just warming up," he said.

I liked him and he was paying attention to me—I should be happy. I went up on pointe in second position.

"Hold my waist to help balance me." His hands were warm even through my shirt. "Not so tight that I can't move."

He loosened his hold. My toe shoes pressed into the carpet, different from the dance floor at the studio. I lifted into an arabesque. Bent my knee—attitude. Billy was better at this than I expected. Maybe skateboarding or bicycling gave him a strong center of gravity.

"I'm going to spin," I told him. I lifted my knee and did a single pirouette, my arm bumping into his shoulder. "Sorry."

He watched me in the mirror, his face still and serious with concentration.

The phone rang, but I didn't care—it was almost never for me. Billy didn't seem to notice. But on the third ring the machine picked up. There was a three-second pause while the outgoing message played, and then the sound of my father's voice froze my heart. I dropped to flat feet and Billy let go of my waist. As if he didn't know what to do with his hands, he put them in his pockets.

My father's voice rumbled through the halls, indistinct, like those recordings of spirits and demons that ghost chasers on TV claim to capture.

"You need to get that?" Billy asked.

I held my breath and tried to make out the words, but I couldn't.

Goose bumps ran up my neck and into my scalp. "No," I said. It was not fair that all my father had to do was speak into a machine and my mood was ruined.

"It's okay," I said, smiling at Billy's reflection. "Hold me up while I lean."

Billy is here, I told myself. *My father is not.*

I lifted into an arabesque and tilted to the right, knowing Billy wouldn't let me fall. He held me hard under the ribs, widening his stance to keep me from slipping. I was not as limber as I used to be, but when I was far enough over, I lifted my other leg until it was fully extended. Billy shifted to counterbalance me.

"Okay, center again," I said, and he pulled me back. Then I tapped his right leg. "Bend this knee. I'm going to sort of dive toward the floor and you hold me up."

"You're gonna do what now?" He looked nervous, but he bent his leg and gripped me tight as I went into a bluebird over his thigh and hooked my crossed feet behind his back. He was trembling a little, but I could extend my arms and throw back my head and he didn't drop me. I didn't want to look at myself in the mirror — it might mess up the fantasy that I looked like I belonged in a ballet company. But out of the corner of my eye I saw the shape of us — my arms extended as if I were flying — and something about that felt great and sad at the same time.

I dropped one foot down, and as I stood up he let go of me. Still we stood facing the mirror. Billy watched my mouth in the reflection as if he were reading my lips when I spoke.

"That's what I can't do by myself," I said. "Thank you."

"Sure."

"It's your turn. What do *you* want?" I asked him.

In the reflection, I was also the backwards me. My father's voice had faded out of the air long ago. I couldn't blame it on him when I felt out of place again.

Billy put his hands in his pockets and thought for a moment, his eyes focused on some place in the distance or maybe in the future.

"I want to walk into my mom's room and have her be awake," he said. "And not sick or anything. Just happy."

My throat tightened. I didn't know what to say. I remembered his brother said their mother had been in the hospital for a long time, but I was afraid to ask about her.

He shook off the idea. "Sorry, you meant what do I want to do with a partner."

The phone rang again and the sound buzzed up my bones like a Taser. I had to clench my fists to keep myself from covering my ears. Billy watched me in the reflection as it rang a second time. He put his hand on my shoulder and I was embarrassed that I was shaking. I just didn't want to hear my father's voice again. Especially not with Billy there. Another ring. Had it always been so loud? Billy was holding both my shoulders now. He began slowly to rub my neck. Not like someone who knows what they're doing—more like someone who has seen movies of people giving back rubs—but it was sweet. And then the next ring cut off and the voice machine never answered. I was relieved—whoever it was had hung up.

I don't think Billy decided to kiss me exactly. But when I turned around we were face-to-face and for half a second our lips touched. So short, like lovers who are just saying hello in a lifetime full of kisses. It caught me by surprise — a soft, warm tease of a touch. His mouth tasted like cinnamon gum, but for some reason I thought, *He should taste like rain.*

"Sorry," said Billy. "I should have asked."

I didn't know what to say or what to do with my hands.

"It's okay." It wasn't like we had never done that before, but it was the first one I remembered.

I sat down on the bed to untie my toe shoes, not looking at him looking at me, when I heard a sound that was familiar and terrible. The kitchen door into the garage had a certain rattle and clunk to it when it opened and closed. Now I turned to him — he seemed like he hadn't heard it. I whispered, "There's a back door in the family room."

One look at my face and he was out of the bedroom in a silent rush. In the hall he turned toward the back of the house and I tried to head my mother off at the dining room.

"Hi," I said, leaning lazily on the corner of the table.

She looked exhausted as she set her purse on a chair, but the next moment her eyes were sharp and she grabbed my arm with an iron grip, hushing me with a finger to her lips. A thumping from the family room had frozen her with fear — a home invader about to break in. Of course I knew it was Billy trying to break out. I'd forgotten to tell him about the wooden dowel that my parents always kept lying in the grooves of the sliding glass door.

Her terror shifted to confusion as she glanced down at my feet. "What is going on here?" she whispered. "Who is in the family room?"

The thumping stopped.

She released my arm. "Go to your room."

And at first I obeyed. I went into my bedroom and closed the door, staying near the crack, listening, but all I heard was my mother on her cell phone speaking quietly—I couldn't make out the words.

And I couldn't stand the suspense—I sneaked out and followed her down the hall. She stopped in the doorway of the family room and I looked around her shoulder to see if Billy had managed to escape or if he was hiding. But no, he was sitting on the sofa, reading our family Bible.

Billy stood up and smiled at her. "Hi."

"Sit down," my mother ordered, so he did. She stood over him. "Reading Scriptures?"

"Sure."

"You came over to read the Bible with my daughter?"

"Would that be okay?" he asked.

She paused but didn't bother answering him. "What do you think of it?"

"What?"

She took the Bible from his hands and folded her arms around it, pressing it to her chest. "What do you think of the Bible?"

He shrugged. "Best book ever written?" He just wanted to please her.

"What part were you reading just now?"

Why was she toying with him? Why didn't she just send him home?

"What part?" said Billy.

"What book of the Bible?" she asked.

"I think it was the third." He looked so lost. "The third part."

"Which Testament?" she asked him.

Billy tilted his head slightly as he tried to read the Bible's cover, half visible in her arms. "American Revised—"

"Do you know how many lies you've told in the last minute?" she asked. "You didn't come here for a Bible study."

"No, I came to see Jenny," he told her. "I like her."

She looked him up and down. "Your shirt is inside out."

"It's not what you think," said Billy.

"Tell me the truth for a change," said my mother.

"Okay." Billy looked her straight in the eye. "I used to like my shirts, but now I think the pictures and jokes are mostly stupid and we don't have money to buy new ones . . . so . . ." He pulled the material away from his chest and let it snap back. "I turn them inside out."

I heard a car in the drive and the sounds of two doors slamming.

"Ask me anything," Billy offered.

"I'll let the police ask the questions from now on," she said. And then the doorbell rang. She had called 911 before cornering Billy in the family room. I ran, beating her to the front door.

"It's a mistake," I blurted out before they could say anything. "I invited a boy from school over and my mom didn't know."

I recognized one of the policemen from church. Officer Redman.

"Everything okay, Jennifer?"

"Yes, yes." I sighed. "I had a friend from school over when Mom was out of the house. We were just talking." If they let me I would have repeated myself for hours.

On his way down the hall toward the family room, Officer Redman spoke into the crackling walkie-talkie on his shoulder strap.

The other officer, whose name was Davis, rocked on his heels, his belt full of weapons clinking and swaying.

"We'll sort it out," he reassured me.

I could hear voices from the back room but couldn't make out what was being said.

"We were just talking," I said again. "I have no idea why she called the police. This is really embarrassing."

Officer Davis nodded without judgment.

"Don't you think I should tell my side of the story?" I asked.

"Everything will be okay," he said. "Just relax."

I couldn't stand not knowing what was being said down the hall. But before I could think of a way to get Officer Davis to let me go to them, Billy came toward us followed by Officer Redman and then my mother. Billy looked ashamed and slinked past me.

"Don't arrest him," I begged.

My mother stayed at the open door with Officer Redman, exchanging a few quiet words as Officer Davis put Billy into the back seat of the waiting police car.

The back window was rolled up and Billy wouldn't look at me. "He was my guest," I said. "He didn't do anything wrong."

"He's not under arrest, honey," said Officer Redman as he went to the driver's door. "We're just taking him home."

And they drove off. My mother watched them until they turned the corner at the end of the block.

"Why did you do that?" I followed her inside. "Why would you call the police on him?"

She waited until the front door was closed tight. "He's been arrested before, you know." Her face was dark and serious as she looked down at my feet again. "Jennifer, did you dance for him?"

I realized then I was still walking around in my toe shoes. "Nothing happened," I told her.

"It's over," she said. "Not another word about it."

Did she mean the argument was over? Or my friendship with Billy?

"And change out of those shoes." She closed herself in the study.

I wanted to slam a door in her face. The rooms in my house felt like prison cells—my bedroom was a coffin. There was not even one corner of space in my house that I felt at home in. I unlaced my toe shoes and left them in piles of ribbon on my floor beside the bed. I went to the family room and lifted the dowel out of the tracks in the sliding glass door. I slid it open as silently as I could and closed it again after me. The sun had hid itself and the sky was pale gray. The breeze was cold, but I needed air. I took deep breaths and remembered Billy talking about lying out on his lawn like a confused animal. I watched how the blades of grass in my own yard curved all in the same direction and fluttered in the wind.

I walked out into the lawn barefoot and sat down before stretching out on my back. The breeze danced my hair around, tickling my face. The sky was a watercolor of grays and whites and lavenders.

Somewhere, I thought, *there's a place where this sky touches down to the ground in every direction instead of going behind houses and trees and power lines. And somewhere the grass grows long with no lawn mowers cutting it and it gets dry and brown without sprinklers, and the land is so flat, you can almost see the curve of the earth if you try.*

I had the strongest feeling that someone should be lying next to me. I turned my head to the side, but there was empty air. There used to someone there, though, I thought. I looked back into the gray.

A drop of rain, invisible until just before it hit my throat, startled me. I have no idea why, but I thought it should have passed through me instead of tapping a wet spot on my skin. As another drop struck my cheek and another my wrist, I lifted my arms and stretched my fingers toward the sky. I tried to move that gray cloud out of the way, but I had no power over it. Of course. If I'd ever had powers, I'd lost them. Another drop hit the corner of my eye like a cold tear.

CHAPTER 13

Helen

Sɪʟᴇɴᴛ ᴜᴘᴏɴ ᴛʜᴇ ɢʀᴀss, she had gazed to her right and to her left in the light rain like Ophelia waiting for a flood. I sat beside her and, in hopes of lifting her spirit, recited poems my first host had written—"The Hearth Cat," "Even Apples Remember," "Below This Leaf."

> *Below this leaf there lies its brother;*
> *Beneath this root one finds another.*
> *And so the layers of time press deep,*
> *Make mud of us all as down we seep.*
> *But do not read your graveyard stone;*
> *You are more than blood and bone.*
> *Up your soul like a fairy flies*
> *And paints its Heaven on the skies.*

I hoped that she had heard me with her inner mind the way my hosts sometimes listened to me while they slept, but it may have been simple chance that when I came to the last line Jenny got herself up and went inside. She took off her wet clothes, showered, dressed herself. She and her mother spoke hardly a word all afternoon and into the evening.

Cathy closed herself in the study or the bedroom and talked on the phone, trying to hide her pain, but the muffled sounds of her tears and anger could be heard through closed doors. I found it disturbing that Cathy abandoned her child for so many hours.

I stayed close to Jenny, told her George MacDonald stories of Curdie, the princess, and the goblins as she brushed out her wet hair, set the table, even as she sat with her mother for an awkward dinner and later helped fold laundry. But I couldn't tell if my poems or stories were truly heard—I sensed no reaction. Frustrated, I swatted at the laundry basket, but neither of them saw it rock.

When her mother left her that evening, retired to the master bedroom to shower, when Jenny was alone and the phone line was free, she stood in the darkened kitchen and called Billy. They spoke but half a minute.

"What did the police do to you?" she asked. She listened, trying with her fingers to rub out a stain on the doorjamb, but it was actually a place where the white paint had chipped away and the dark wood showed through. Then she whispered, "Okay." And, "Monday at ten." She looked down the hall as the sound of the shower shut off. "Don't you have to be at school?" she asked him. Jenny stepped back away from the doorway and hid in the shadows. "The main branch?" Then she laughed, stifled the sound with her hand, and hung up.

She crept back into the living room, where Cathy joined her, wearing pajamas under a long sweater and her hair wet around the edges. It was rare to see the woman dressed so informally. And without makeup she looked young and lost.

They watched television, a concert of Christian music that Cathy said Jenny could stay up for if she wanted to; a baritone sang a gospel song older even than I was, a full choir performed an arrangement of "God Bless America," a boy's chorus sang "This Little Light of Mine." Cathy held a cup of tea she never drank—her eyes were focused not on the television screen but at the floor below it. Jenny didn't seem to be watching the program either, except that one of the advertisements made her sit up straight.

It was a commercial for a credit card that would, it was implied, be accepted anywhere on the planet. A montage of famous places was accompanied by romantic strains of cellos and oboes. The Great Sphynix in Egypt, a white beach and blue lagoon in Greece, the Lincoln Memorial, the Taj Mahal, the Golden Gate Bridge, Big Ben, the Great Wall of China, the Eiffel Tower.

Jenny stood up. "I'm going to bed." Perhaps on other nights she might have asked permission to go to her room, but this evening she turned without saying good night to her mother and walked out of the room and down the hall. Cathy seemed not to notice.

I followed Jenny into her room, where she closed the door. She walked to her bed, but instead of sitting or lying down, she crouched beside it on the floor and began to cry as if her heart had been shattered. She reached up and took one of the pillows off her bed, holding it to her face.

I sat on the rug beside her and tried to stroke her hair or rub her back, but I was having trouble keeping my spectral body together. I felt nervous and vaporous. With each of Jenny's sobs I shifted in the air, a little closer, now away, like a cloud of gnats.

"Hush," I whispered. "Poor thing."

She cried into the pillow until I thought she might become ill.

"Get into bed now," I told her.

After a few moments she took a hitching breath and crawled up onto her mattress, still clutching the pillow.

"Rest your head and I'll sing you a song," I whispered. I was relieved that she seemed to be sensing my message — by and by she stretched out and put the pillow under her head, wiped her eyes on her sleeves, and gave a heavy sigh.

I sang a folk song I'd sung to my own little girl a hundred times — the one about the rolling river. Soon Jenny's eyes were closed and her breaths came smooth and far between. Tears had dried on her face in delicate salt lines. Her hair fanned out on one side of the pillow.

"Why are you sad?" I asked her.

I didn't expect her to answer, but from her throat came the faintest sound of question, as if she hadn't understood me properly. It gave me a thrill to think she might have actually heard my question in her sleep.

"Why were you crying?" I asked.

Then the faintest sound of regret from deep in her dream. And four words, "I used to fly."

I wanted so for her to say it again so I could be sure I'd heard correctly — she used to fly, and that was sad.

I sat on the edge of her bed all night long, but she didn't speak again. After watching her in silence for a time, I decided to slip back to heaven and tell James that I had finally spoken with Jenny. To tell him that from now on I was sure it would be easy to talk to her. I was certain I could visit James and be back before Jenny woke up in the morning.

I thought about the last place I'd seen James, in a shaded wood beside a clover-covered tree trunk. I pictured the quality of light, the scent of damp earth, the piano music, a lilting melody, a folk song I couldn't place, sweet even in its minor keys.

And in the same way it happened when I neared Jenny, as I closed in on heaven everything in front of me thinned into converging lines. Jenny's bedroom and the garden outside her window and the hills beyond her neighborhood flattened like a sketch of themselves drawn on a sheet of paper and contracted into black and white, ink on a blank page, but then it stopped. I couldn't stretch it any further, and try as I might I couldn't slide into it between the shadow and the light.

I was frightened for a moment, but fear had not helped me find heaven the first time. Then I was angry — how could God deny me entry when I'd had such a charitable motive for leaving? The truth was, I realized, that I had made a promise to come back to Jenny and be her guardian until the troubles I brought her had been calmed. If I broke my word, it seemed I would not be traveling back to James.

I was trapped in the land of the Quick until I fulfilled my promise to Jenny.

⌒

Because I had borrowed Jenny's body for only six days, and since I had claimed her on a Sunday afternoon, I had never been to church with her family. Now I trailed after mother and daughter into a back pew. Cathy didn't admit to it, but I believe she made sure we arrived a little late to the church service so that she would not be stopped on the way in and have to answer questions about Jenny's father leaving.

The sanctuary appeared to make Jenny uncomfortable. Her bones seemed to stiffen, her muscles to contract in a subtle way, as if she were preparing to be struck. Tolerantly she adjusted herself to Cathy's nagging — pulled her skirt down closer to her knee, tucked a lock of hair behind her ear.

There were things about Jenny's church that I found familiar — the iron chandeliers were so like the ones from my childhood church, only these were fitted with artificial candles and electric bulbs. The dark wooden pews, worn smooth where a thousand hands had rested, seemed familiar, as well. And the carpets and pew cushions, a maroon brocade made murky with years of wear, bothered me most. Even the most mundane memories, if drawn from a deep-enough well, can chill the heart. The baskets of flowers on either side of the altar in Jenny's church were almost identical to those at my mother's funeral — lilies in white wicker. And the carvings on the wooden gate leading up to the altar, they were exactly like ones from my youth. I was unprepared for recollections from my girlhood: candlelit Christmas services, sunny Easters, brooding autumn Sundays when thunder could be heard over the groan of the pump organ. The scents and emotions made me ache, but I cherished them too. I could almost taste the metal cup and feel the icy water of the well in the churchyard, smell the mint that grew below the well stones.

I moved closer to Jenny on the pew. I wanted to cover her like a blanket.

She looked pale, as if she'd been bleached into a faded version of herself. The organist was playing a prelude, a chain of old hymns slowed to a merciless dirge meant to stretch until the Judgment Day, it seemed. As the hymn "This Is My Father's World" changed into "Leaning on the Everlasting Arm," I began to see glimpses from my childhood acquaintances scattered through the congregation—a head of ash-colored hair to our left, broad shoulders in a black suit a few rows in front of us, a sharp jaw turning halfway toward me. But these were not my people. My people had been gone for decades, even the babies, grown, withered and cold, dead and in the ground fifty years back or more.

But I am still here, I thought. *And Jenny is here.*

The prelude had finally ceased and the pastor was greeting the congregation and making announcements. The pews were set with paper bulletins every few feet—Jenny took one and stared at the cover, a photograph of a field of gold wheat under a blue sky. Across the curved stalks of grain a line of Scripture was printed in slanted cursive: *The fruit of the Spirit is love — Galatians 5:22.*

As Jenny studied the picture, the pink began to return to her cheeks. Cathy was reading ahead in the order of service and must have expected the same of her daughter. "Jen," she whispered.

But Jenny was rubbing the picture of a field with her thumb, tilting it toward the light as if she could not decipher its meaning.

CHAPTER 14

Jenny

My mother reached over and flipped my bulletin open for me. The organ started up again: "Come Thou Font of Every Blessing."

I had the feeling that someone was standing in the aisle watching and waiting for me to move over and make room for him or her to sit, but when I looked, there was no one there.

I sat frozen, trying to hold the bulletin still, but it was vibrating. The picture of the empty field meant something—I just hadn't figured out what it was yet. The picture was vibrating to the rhythm of my heart pounding. It was stupid to feel like someone watching me was unusual—I was in church, so of course people would look at me.

Then the page I held stopped shaking as if an invisible hand had gripped it. The tension pulling gently on the paper from the top was unmistakable. When my mother handed me the hymnal, it ruined the moment. Whatever was holding my bulletin let go.

"Wake up," my mother whispered, and slipped the order of worship out of my fingers, setting it on the pew as the congregation stood up to sing. I got to my feet and sang along, but I was spooked by the sensation of someone's breath right beside my shoulder where there was no one standing. If it was a draft, why did it come and go? And it couldn't really be someone singing—the breath would be hot, and this air was cool.

Then came a pressure on my hand, the one that held up the hymnal. I switched the book to my other hand and flexed those fingers. It was as if static electricity were running through my veins instead of blood. And for no good reason, the skin of that hand smelled like flowers, not lotion or perfume, but fresh flowers.

I wasn't paying attention to the pastor when he invited the congregation to sit. My mother snapped her fingers and I dropped to the pew, the last one in the room to take a seat. She handed me my bulletin again and tapped the page—we were supposed to be reading along with the prayer, but I couldn't act like everything was normal. Something unnatural was happening here even if I was the only one who recognized it.

I could see, from the corner of my eye, that there was someone sitting beside me just far back enough so that I couldn't make out the face. I knew if I turned it would be gone.

Whatever it was, it was communicating without making sound. Maybe I was going crazy, but I was in church—people have had impossible things happen to them in churches for centuries. Maybe this was a miracle, an angel.

Or maybe there was something wrong with my brain—I had amnesia. Maybe now I was having hallucinations.

"What's wrong?" my mother whispered.

I couldn't say, "I'm delusional." I glanced at her and smiled.

As I faced the front of the sanctuary, sure enough, I felt the visitor was still there. I took up the hymnal again, slowly, making sure I didn't move too quickly. I didn't want to scare it away. I found the song that the organ was playing in my hymnal. I ran my finger along the line of text I'd heard in my head. Then my eyes wandered to the upper corner of the page where the topics were listed.

Ghost, it said.

Actually the topic was Holy Ghost, but I felt as if someone was running an invisible finger under the second word.

I had the most bizarre sensations fighting in my chest. What if this wasn't an angel but a ghost? My heart was going crazy and my stomach was cramping with fear. At the same time, I felt special for being chosen and clever to have figured out how to communicate with this whatever-it-was.

I flipped to the back of the hymnal where the topics were listed. If this was how we could talk, I had questions.

There were dozens of key words to choose from: *comfort, praise, advent, forgiveness, heaven, grace,* and (among others) *the Holy Ghost/Holy Spirit*. I felt my gaze pulled to one of the hymns listed and started turning pages.

My mother frowned at me. "What are you doing?"

"Reading hymns," I told her. How could she find fault in that?

I found the right page and ran my finger along the lines following that odd little static electricity buzz I'd felt before: *Come, Holy Ghost, for moved by thee the prophets wrote and spoke; Unlock the truth, Thyself the key; unseal the sacred book.*

Be moved by me, someone was saying. *I unseal myself for you.*

I was so excited, my face prickled, and my pulse was turning into a trill. On the topics page I chose another hymn that felt like it was chosen for me. I found the page and read the lines that buzzed: *Word of God and inward light, wake my spirit, clear my sight . . . Kindle every high desire; perish self in thy pure fire.*

Wake to me, it was saying. It almost seemed as if the word *desire* was being lit by a penlight. I could hardly sit still.

"Jennifer," my mother hissed at me. "Where's your bulletin?" The congregation read along with a Scripture lesson in the order of service. My mother lifted the hymnal right out of my hands and flipped it shut, setting it on the pew on the other side of her where I could not reach it.

How humiliating to be treated like a five-year-old, I thought, but as soon as she looked away, I gently slipped the Bible from the back of the pew in front of me and set it in my lap.

Part of my brain knew everyone had stood up for singing the Doxology, but it was a world away from what was happening to me. I turned to the back of the Bible and found the subject lists. Holding my breath I searched, waiting to be guided.

"What are you doing?" my mother snapped at me.

I didn't mean to lie, exactly — I just said what I thought she wanted to hear. "I'm reveling in the word of God."

The offering plates were being passed now, but I had plenty of time before I would have to hand a plate to anyone. This was more important. I was creating a new language with someone or something otherworldly.

I began by running her finger down the subject list, feeling for passages that vibrated — but all I felt was a pressure around my head. I stopped, shut the Bible. Still I felt squeezed. I let go of the Bible and it fell open naturally (or so it seemed) across my lap. The pressure was gone, so I looked into the two pages that had come to me by accident.

Hebrews. I dropped my hand on the page and read the line above my fingertips: *Don't forget to be kind to strangers. For some who have done this have entertained angels without realizing it.*

I didn't know I'd made a sound, but my mother shot me a look. I passed the offering plate she handed me to the waiting usher.

I paused until my mother stopped glaring at me. So weird to be watching both her from the corner of my eye on the right while I still had that vague shadow on my left back in the edge of my vision. When it seemed safe, I slowly pressed the Bible closed between my palms and meant to let it open randomly, but it landed at my feet with a clunk.

"What's got into you?" my mother whispered.

As I reached down to pick up the Bible, I noticed Mrs. Caine in a pew across the aisle watching me. I spread the Bible out on my lap just as it had fallen, open to the book of Ruth. My finger dropped onto the page:

> Whither thou goest, I will go; and where thou lodgest, I will lodge: thy people shall be my people, and thy God my God: Where thou diest, will I die, and there will I be buried: the LORD do so to me, and more also, if ought but death part thee and me.

I could hear the drone of the pastor beginning his sermon but not the words. My head was full of loud silence, like the running of a stream. My heart was full too—I was happy in a way that didn't make sense. Like how the day before it made no sense that I felt more at home lying in the grass outside my house than I did in my own bedroom. Like how I fell apart during a stupid credit card commercial on TV. The night before I felt like I was missing someone I'd left behind, and now someone had come to see me.

CHAPTER 15

Helen

Jenny smiled to herself, glanced around again, searching for me, I was sure. You would think I would be the one to explain how this language worked, but it was a mystery. Whether my desire to speak with her had bent the binding of the book and forced a certain page to fall open and then guided her hand to find words that made sense to her or whether we were only imagining it, I had no idea. This had not been in my plan—I'd never done such a thing with any of my other hosts. But Jenny dropped the Bible on the floor again, intentionally this time. The thud reverberated through the sanctuary. The woman across the aisle who had been watching made an audible gasp. She was one of the ladies from Cathy's women's group. She stared at Jenny as if the girl had shouted out a blasphemy. Cathy swooped down and snatched the Bible away, stuffed it under her purse where Jenny could not reach it.

Did she think she could keep me from talking to my girl that easily? I tapped the bulletin lying on the pew. It didn't move, but Jenny picked it up and opened it all the same. I pointed to one word after another, jumping around from this line to that. Jenny ran her finger along the print, through prayers and Scripture quotes and hymn titles, following my lead, and we shared (I hoped) a poem of my constructing: *I — will — protect — thee — let — not — your — heart — be — sorrow.*

When I couldn't find the phrases I needed, I placed my finger on the white space in the middle fold of the bulletin. Jenny's finger glided into the blank place between my finger and a staple and stopped. She stared at the page, her breaths coming in shallow puffs.

Leaning toward her ear, I whispered, "Please forgive me for leaving you alone in such a dark place. I'm here now, and I won't let anyone hurt you."

Her whisper was so soft, Cathy couldn't have heard her unless she'd pressed her ear to the girl's lips. "Is it you?" Jenny asked.

"Yes," I whispered. I couldn't find the word in the bulletin. I wrote the letters gently on her arm. *Yes.*

Jenny nodded ever so slightly.

"Ghost," she whispered.

Again I wrote with my finger on the back of her hand a *Y* for *Yes.*

She shuddered, I thought, with equal parts fear and joy. My spirit answered in kind, flickering with nervous excitement.

I thought I felt someone watching me, which is an uncommon sensation for a spirit, but when I turned I saw that the woman across the aisle was studying Jenny. Her gaze went right through me. Behind this woman's eyes I saw an unsettling mix of concern and pleasure. And under her eyes, a shadow.

At the end of the service Cathy took Jenny's hand and tried

to hurry out the back way before anyone spoke to them. A plump woman with a Noah's ark sweater blocked the side door and began smothering Cathy with sympathy. I paced around them, impatient to be alone with Jenny. The woman asked Jenny to volunteer in the babies' room so she could take Cathy to the ladies' lounge for a talk.

"Oh, here's Brad," said the woman. "Honey, why don't you walk Jennifer to the nursery?"

I stayed between this boy and Jenny, though he seemed perfectly harmless. He was thin and dressed as neat as a missionary. He chatted, oblivious that Jenny was not listening.

"If you ever need anyone to talk to," he said. "Or pray with." Jenny didn't seem to have heard him. "Do you think you'll want to go to the Harvest Dance?" he asked.

"What?" She didn't appear to comprehend.

"I should ask your father if I can invite you." Brad realized his faux pas. "I mean your mother, I guess. I think my mom already talked to her."

How I wanted to swat him away as I would a horsefly. Jenny swung open the half door under the sign CHERUBS' NEST and slammed it shut without inviting him in.

"I could come by your house," he told her, leaning on the door shelf, but Jenny only smiled at him weakly and turned away. "I'll just call."

The nursery was full and loud. A dozen babies under the age of two sat, crawled, rolled, and toddled around the rainbow carpet. Half were laughing, half were fussing. No one napping. My heart clutched at the sight—every round face reminded me of my own child.

A tiny woman with thick spectacles was taping a torn page in a picture book. "Are you helping with second service?" she asked Jenny. "You're a lifesaver." She came over and put an arm around Jenny's waist, gave her a squeeze, and whispered, "I'm so sorry about your father."

News travels swiftly among the church ladies—some things never change.

The woman adjusted her glasses. "The usual sunbeams are here. Russell's got a runny nose, but everyone else is full of spunk. Darryl Ann needs changing. Would you be a dear?"

A dimpled one-year-old waddled over to us, glanced at me without interest, and wrapped her arms around Jenny's legs, grinning with four tiny teeth.

Jenny sighed. "Come on, you." She swung the baby onto her hip and headed to the next door in the hallway. A utility closet had been remade into a diapering station with paper diapers in three sizes, boxes of wipes, powders, lotions, and a large lidded trash can.

It might have been the way the child held the back of Jenny's dress in her fist, or the way her leg swung as it dangled, or the size of the closet, but I imagined I could smell the baby's sweaty hair and milk-sweet breath. I felt the weight of her, the warmth of her on my side, though she was not in my own arms. Impossible.

Jenny diapered the child as I watched, teasing her to laughter by tickling her in the ribs, and I was struck by how I imagined I could taste the salt as Jenny pretended to bite one chubby hand.

Maybe it was because I had been inside Jenny, tasted an apple with her tongue, kissed James with her lips, breathed through her, and smelled the sweet foresty pine of James's hair. I had controlled Jenny's every joint and muscle, looked through the lens of a camera using her eyes. I recalled it so crisply, as if it were still true. Even now I thought I felt the shape and vibration of wearing her flesh.

If I knew what it was like to be under her skin, I thought, *couldn't I induce her to feel what it was like to be me?*

It wasn't as if I told her how I died, but the flood came all the same. That it appeared to us both should have come as a surprise to me, but it felt perfectly natural.

The little room shook as if a cannon had fired into the wall. Jenny snatched up the baby and held her against her chest. The familiar howl of the storm swelled from every direction. I felt somehow vindicated when Jenny seemed to hear it too. She turned around in a circle, confused.

And then the lights went out.

"No way!" Jenny's voice went fierce to cover the shock. She held the whimpering baby close to her heart, just as I had.

Jenny felt her way to the door and tried to push it open, but something was blocking it. I knew what it was, of course, but I could sense Jenny's thoughts—a bookcase or some other heavy piece of furniture? She threw her shoulder against the door, but it didn't budge. No, not a bookcase. There was a fallen tree against the cellar door. My cellar, my tree.

"Hello?" Jenny called. "Can I get a hand here?"

It's all right, I told her. *Don't be scared.*

And then the water came. Rushing under the door, a roaring river of it. Jenny shrieked. The baby let loose, crying in earnest. But this little girl couldn't hear the storm or see the flood, could she? I supposed it was Jenny's fear that was upsetting her.

Jenny held the little girl on one hip, away from the door, then banged with her fist. "Hey! A pipe broke or something!"

I knew the water could not drown her—I wasn't afraid. I was thrilled. She was attuned to me, powerfully. My spirit swelled with joy.

Jenny shrieked as a branch broke through the door with splinters flying. Water shot in at her face. "Somebody help!" Jenny kicked the door. "We're trapped in here!"

Icy water swirled around our ankles. *Do you understand what's happening?* I asked her. *I'm telling you my story.*

"Help!" Jenny yelled, guarding the baby from the phantom spray of water.

When the door swung in at us, the light from the hall blinded me for a moment. I turned to Jenny. She swallowed back a scream and blinked.

"What in the world is going on in here?" the short woman asked.

The moment had passed. The water was gone. No tree limb stuck through the door.

"I pushed and pushed but the door wouldn't open," said Jenny.

"It opens inward, honey." The woman studied her.

"And the lights went out," said Jenny.

The woman reached over and flipped the light switch on. The room was perfectly bright. "Seems fine now."

The woman adjusted her glasses then held out her arms to the weeping baby. "Did Jenny scare you? You're all right, doodle bug."

The child flung herself at the woman and Jenny was left alone with me in the changing room, breathing hard.

I moved close to her shoulder to calm her. We were one now. We could feel each other's pain and fear. She had let me in.

I will never quit you, not by the threat of hell or the promise of heaven, I told her. *I am yours to command.*

CHAPTER 16

Helen

A HYMNAL OR A BIBLE IS A LOVELY TEXT, but I was so looking forward to talking with Jenny using a novel or a collection of poetry. I'd always had a special love for books. I liked all kinds—children's stories, song books, poetry, histories—but my favorites were novels. Our town didn't have a library and when I was a child my parents did not own books, so I was forced to borrow them from neighbors and friends, sell what I could to buy them—my plum preserves bartered a slightly used copy of *Ivanhoe* once. I never stole one, but when I was sixteen I did trade a tablecloth for *Little Dorrit*. A tearful confession of love for which you have waited three hundred pages was much better than eating off white lace.

I sat in the back seat of Jenny's car on the way home from church, my mind swimming with wonderful stories, any one of which I would love to read for the first time all over again along with Jenny. I could hardly sit still in the car—to think I could re-read any books we chose, that I helped Jenny choose, running my finger under certain words and phrases to communicate with her all my deepest thoughts. Impatiently I flew through the closed door as the car turned onto Jenny's street—I rushed into the house right through the kitchen wall.

How could I be so forgetful? I floated from room to room and found no novels at all. There were manuals and cookbooks, Bibles and catalogs, Christian magazines, audiobooks, but no Dickens or Hugo or Austen. I had discovered this tragedy the first night I slept in Jenny's home. Even at Billy's house James had hidden a book of Robert Frost poetry under the bed. But Jenny's house was a wasteland. I longed for the book-heavy homes of my past hosts.

I paced in the hallway having searched every room for novels—perhaps the book bag she took to school might still have school library books in it? But I found it sitting closed beside her desk and I couldn't open it. I waited there for Jenny in her bedroom. Perhaps there were no volumes of Robert Louis Stevenson or Emily Brontë to be found, but I used to tell my daughter stories from memory, paraphrasing scenes without looking at the books—*The Water Babies* and *Jane Eyre*—while I bathed her or as she watched me hang up the wash or as I nursed her by the hearth.

When Jenny walked in I practically pounced on her, but all the things I wanted to tell her leapt up in my mind at once and confused me.

Although some of my plans to contact Jenny had been ill-conceived, she and I had been bound by an invisible cord now. Clearly she had felt my thoughts through the printed word—she'd seen and heard my death scene. I was confident that if I spoke to her as she slept tonight, she would understand me.

How vexing that it was only midday. I paced back and forth in and out of the bedroom wall as Jenny changed from church clothes to simple cotton slacks and shirt—she wrapped herself in an oversize sweater as if still cold after the spectral flood I had shared with her. Jenny sat at her vanity table and began to brush her hair.

So many things to tell her. I had abandoned her studies — embarrassing, but not dangerous. I must tell her about how Mitch had banned James (well, Billy) from being alone in their house with me. Billy wouldn't remember that. Oh, yes, and I had said some rather shocking things to the church ladies — I was angry that they seemed to think they knew who was in heaven and who wasn't. I even got out of Cathy's car in a strange neighborhood and accused Cathy of driving Jenny away from her life. I told her the truth, which of course she would never believe, that I was not her daughter. Oh, and I couldn't forget to tell her what went on in the principal's office — I was sent to the office, where her parents were waiting to confront Mr. Brown, who they thought had seduced me. A sickening misunderstanding — Jenny needed to know what was said.

I stood behind her as she sat at the vanity. Or maybe, I thought, I should start explaining it all by beginning with the story of how I met James.

Jenny froze with her brush in midair. She was staring into the looking glass, but it wasn't the image of her face that made her stop and think — it was the sight of the back of her head reflected in the mirrors on her closet doors.

⌒

Cathy had agreed to meet with the pastor and did not want to talk about Jenny's father in front of her and would not leave her at home alone. Which is probably why it only took a few minutes for Jenny to convince her mother to let her study at the main branch library that day.

Cathy handed over her phone. "Call me when you're done," she said, as Jenny climbed out of the car. "Until twelve at the church and after that at home."

"Okay." Jenny swung her book bag over one shoulder.

"And don't talk to strangers."

"I won't. I have lunch money. I'll be fine."

Do you think I would let anything happen to her? I said, but Cathy didn't hear.

Finally she left us on the sidewalk in front of the library. Jenny waited just inside the entrance, trying not to pace, checking the clock every half minute, glancing out the windows in the front doors. I remembered how the last few minutes before I would see James again always felt like hours.

Don't fret, I told her. But I did wonder if he would come. Life is complicated and there were scores of obstacles that might hinder him.

But Billy ran up the stairs at last and shoved open the doors at 10:33. Jenny's shoulders relaxed.

"How did you know I would wait for you?" she asked him.

"You're a nice person," he said. "You wouldn't just ditch somebody."

Where are your manners? I scolded him.

"Sorry I was late," he said. "When you tell your mom you want to study at the library I bet she believes you. Not so easy convincing Mitch. But I promised not to jump bail."

"What does that mean?" she asked.

He waved the question away. "It's an in-joke."

"So, what do you want to do?" Jenny asked.

He gave her a baffled expression and motioned toward the cavernous room beyond the information desk. "Study."

I followed a few paces behind as Jenny and Billy went in search of an empty table. All the private study rooms were taken. They squeezed into a single carrel, partially screened off by a kind of desk blinder. They sat in plastic chairs pressed side by side—Jenny held her book bag in her lap.

"What do you want to study?" she asked.

Billy pulled out a few pages of folded notebook paper from the back pocket of his jeans. "Something I found last night."

I don't know what I had expected, but the sight of those pages, even before they were opened, covered in my writing, startled me so that the cord to the blinds beside me began to swing.

"What is it?" Jenny spread out the papers on the small desk.

"I think somebody lived our lives for us during the time we can't remember." His voice was quiet, but inside I could feel him spinning with excitement. "See, I think this comes first." He turned over the top page and tapped on the word *haunt.*

I gripped Jenny's shoulder, willing her not to be frightened.

She took the paper slowly. "Who would want to live our lives?"

"Someone who needed a body," said Billy. "Who didn't have a body of their own anymore."

"A ghost?"

"Use your library voice," Billy whispered.

"Sorry," she whispered back. Billy watched her staring at the page.

"I found it in a box under my bed with some other stuff that wasn't mine. See?" He took the papers back, ordered them, and ran his finger down the first one. "Two different kinds of handwriting."

Jenny stared as if Billy had uncovered an ancient treasure.

"Two ghosts," said Billy, "passing notes in class." He was grinning now, and I sensed it was not because the idea of ghosts delighted him, but because he had bound himself to Jenny with a story she would find utterly compelling.

"I think this is him, the one who was me." Billy moved his finger under the words as he read. "*Where have you been? Please don't be afraid. I would be a friend to you.*"

James's handwriting was stylish and angled, and even though Billy's inflections were a little different as he read aloud, the tone of his voice was so like James.

Billy read on. "*Follow me after class. I long to speak with you again.*"

"Again," Jenny echoed. That was all that was written on the front of the first page, but he turned it over and there was an entire page of writing, alternating between that jaunty hand and my small cursive lettering.

"*How long have you been Light?*" Billy read. "That's still him. And also this word — *Which?*" He leaned close to Jenny as he whispered. "And here's your ghost." Billy pointed to the next word and she read it aloud.

"*Write.*" Jenny shivered.

A thrill coiled through me remembering this scene. We couldn't speak aloud to each other during class because James kept forgetting that he could be heard — we had to write out our first questions and answers.

Billy went on reading what James had written and Jenny read my part.

"*That was amazing,*" he read.

She read, "*How true.*"

And Billy read, "*Why do you haunt this place?*"

Jenny asked him, "This place? The school?"

"Keep reading," he urged.

Then Jenny read, "*I don't. I'm attached to Mr. Brown.*"

My spirit tingled with joy.

"The English teacher," Jenny whispered.

Billy smiled and read, "*Why?*"

Jenny read the one word answer. "*Literature.*" She blinked and swallowed before she read on. "*He's my host.*"

"*Lucky man,*" Billy read.

A woman pushing a cart of books passed by the study carrel and Billy leaned in even closer to Jenny as she whispered the next question I had asked James that day. "*Have you ever seen Billy's spirit since you took his body?*"

Jenny looked at him, amazed. I had been standing behind her chair, resting my hand on her shoulder. But now I felt shy. I stepped back and stood halfway through the window, but still I watched and listened—I couldn't help myself. It was a peculiar sensation, to have one's most intimate love notes recited as if they were lines from a play.

"*Only once,*" Billy whispered as he read. "*I thought I saw him watching me for a moment the first night I slept in his room.*" As if it was the most natural of gestures, he laid his hand on Jenny's arm. "Is this freaky or what?"

Without answering Jenny read, "*Did he speak to you?*"

And Billy read the reply. "*Alas, no.*"

I read the next line along with Jenny. "*So you go home to Mr. Blake's family at night?*"

Memories of Billy's house made me nostalgic for my few days with James. It was a sad home, in many ways, no mother or father, few books, unkept grass and no flowers, empty beer bottles and piles of half-read newspapers. But it was also the place where James and I slept in the same bed; even before I had a body, my spirit lay beside him. I even loved the garage with the rusty patchwork car in which we drove to school one day, and the kitchen where I watched Billy bite into an apple, something I had been deprived of for more than a century.

Billy read James's remark about this home as if he was not in the least insulted, "*Such as it is.*"

Then Jenny read the two words, "*No room.*" She shook her head, but Billy grinned and placed the other page over the one in her hands.

Jenny smiled back. "They ran out of space to write on the first piece of paper, didn't they? This is so weird." The beginning line on the new page was James, so Jenny waited for Billy to start.

"*Sorry,*" he read, then the next word made my heart jump. "*Helen.*"

I knew what we'd written. I remembered it perfectly, but still it made me ache. I began to weep at the sound.

"*Don't go home with Mr. Brown,*" Billy read. "*Come with me.*"

"Wow." Jenny covered her cheeks and read my words, "*I'm afraid of leaving my host.*"

"*You must've changed hosts before,*" Billy read.

Hosts was just a word to these children, one they barely understood. But to me it was like a fan unfolding, recollections of my beloved ones: my Saint searching the cairns of books in her tiny home for a certain volume of Homer; my Knight dressing for the theater before his great mirror, struggling with his stiff collar. My Playwright falling drunk onto the bed he shared with dozens of half-read books, their spines cracking under him. My Poet in his dark office, hunched in the light of a single lamp, his gray hair fallen over his spectacles, rereading a poem about Zeus. Mr. Brown driving with his elbow out the open window of his car, looking so young and as if he would live forever, the briefcase on the seat beside him hiding his unfinished novel.

Then Billy read, "*Help me.*"

CHAPTER 17

Helen

Jenny turned the page over, but that was the last entry. She was trembling. I came to stand behind her again and rested my hand gently on her back to quell her fears.

Billy seemed uncertain now, took his hands off her arm. "Are you scared?" he asked. "They're ghosts . . ."

"I'm not afraid of them," she said. "I think one was trying to talk to me yesterday."

I tensed, my spirit rippling with nerves. I wasn't sure I wanted her to share our experience with Billy.

"Really?" He watched her face, fascinated. "What happened?"

Jenny folded up the pages. "It's hard to describe. But I think maybe one of them drowned," she said. "I don't know."

"Was it Helen?"

I squeezed her shoulder, but she made no sign of feeling my presence this time.

"At first I thought it was someone I'd met, maybe, during the time I can't remember." Jenny handed the pages back to Billy. "But he was probably just something I dreamed."

"A ghost tried to talk to you?" he asked. "How?"

"I could have imagined it," she said. "I've had a really strange week."

"Tell me about it," Billy whispered. He returned the pages to his pocket and pulled out a small, thin book from his other back pocket and held it out to her. "And it's about to get even stranger."

It had a soft cover, plain black, no title.

"Is that a journal?" asked Jenny.

"Sketchbook." He opened it to the first page, where there was a beautiful pencil depiction of what looked like a wooden ladder and a kind of carpenter's table. I recognized it but apparently they did not.

"Did you draw this?" Jenny touched the paper tentatively.

"No. Someone living in my room did it with my pencils and left it under my bed." Billy turned to the second page. Another drawing, this one of the tree under which James and I had shared a picnic. "It's the tree from school, across from the cafeteria."

Jenny nodded. He kept turning the pages, five in all, not in chronological order of when James and I had visited them, but laid out as if James had been recalling random moments from our handful of days together. The third was a phone booth (the one where James and I spoke — he was holding the receiver to his ear, but he was speaking to me, and I was inches from him though invisible to everyone else); the next a sketch of two empty chairs and a table in the school library (where we did Billy's homework assignment together); and the last was a drawing of a face, not mine, and not Jenny's, but somehow both.

"Is that her?" Jenny asked out loud. An elderly man with an armful of art books was passing their carrel and stopped as if Jenny had spoken to him. Billy motioned her to hush. But the man did not move away—instead he stood a few feet from them, reading book covers in the adjacent aisle.

Billy turned to the next page in the journal and snatched up one of the little pencils from the shelf where scratch paper is left in small trays. On the blank page he wrote: *She would have looked like you, right?*

Jenny slipped the pencil out of his fingers and under this line wrote: *What should we do now?*

Billy smiled, and instead of taking the pencil from her, he wrapped his hand around hers and moved her hand, just as I had done with James when I was Light. Jenny read the words they had written together: *Field trip.*

$\sim$

They boarded a city bus and sat together near the back where no one was close enough to overhear their conversation. I sat across the aisle trying not to think about riding this kind of bus with James's arm around me—it made me miss him too much.

"What if we get caught?" Jenny asked.

"Caught at school during school hours?"

"But my mother tells me I've been pulled out," she said. "I'm going to be homeschooled."

Billy was distracted by some thought he didn't share. "Yeah, Mitch is sticking me in night school if I get probation."

"Because of me?" Jenny looked guilty. "Is that another in-joke? Does probation mean your brother grounded you?"

"No." Billy shrugged it off. "It's a long story you do not want to hear."

I followed them a few paces behind as they were dropped off a block from the high school and as they made their way onto the campus through the rows of lockers during passing period. Billy found that his locker combination still worked, and there was a soft hooded jacket rumpled up at the bottom. Jenny put it on over her prim, acorn-button cardigan, and Billy carried her book bag over his shoulder.

No one paid them any attention and they remained inconspicuous, staying near the bicycle racks until the second bell rang and the paths between buildings were empty again.

"So." Billy walked up to the tree in front of the cafeteria and looked around. "This is the tree he drew." Jenny scanned the lawn and looked up into the branches. All I could think of was the glory of tasting fresh orange and the crunch of an apple, the familiar softness of a boiled egg, things I had not eaten in 130 years until I sat under this tree with James.

"Do you get any hits off this place?" Billy asked.

"Hits?" Jenny smiled out from under the black hood. "I'm not a medium."

"You told me a ghost was trying to talk to you," said Billy. "Can you try saying something to them right now?"

I bristled at this childish game. *I am not a Halloween party prank*, I snapped at him, but he was oblivious.

A woman in kitchen whites came out of the cafeteria and frowned at Billy and Jenny. "Why aren't you in class?" she called.

"We're going," Billy called back. He pulled the notebook pages from his back pocket and waved them at her in a blur. "We got hall passes."

The woman propped the door open with a wooden wedge and left them alone again.

They gave up trying to conjure a spirit at the tree and moved on to the phone booth beside the gymnasium. My soul fluttered with nerves at this place. It was where I first learned James's name and where we shared our secrets, my bondage to hosts, his imprisonment to the land where his childhood home had once stood.

Billy opened the squeaking door and stepped inside. He looked for clues, but all the scratched and painted messages were from others and in a quite different tone than any note James or I might have left behind. Jenny stepped up to the opening and looked up and around through the cracked glass.

"Maybe one of them called the other from here," Billy suggested.

Jenny shrugged. "Does it even work anymore?"

Billy lifted the receiver and clicked the button hidden underneath.

I had the odd idea, just then, that only Billy's fingerprints would be found on the phone, if a detective were working to piece together the mystery of my days with James. For our conversation in this tiny booth was before I had fingers.

They paused at the school library window, but Jenny grabbed Billy's sleeve, holding him back. "There are too many people," she said. "The librarian knows me too well."

For a moment I thought, *I have spent more hours here than either of you.* Remembering how I had helped James compose an essay as if he were Billy, sitting at a table in this little library, made me miss James again. But as I tried to recall the last time I had seen him, heaven did not come into focus in my mind. I wanted to remember the last thing he said to me before I left heaven to find Jenny, but there was only silence. This bothered me so much that as I dragged behind Billy and Jenny toward the auditorium it felt as if I were wading through a drift of snow.

The double doors had been left propped open even though there didn't seem to be anyone inside. The house was dark, but there was a pool of light on the stage and a can of paint and two wooden chairs nearby sitting on a tarp. Nothing else.

Billy paused at the back of the house, perhaps listening to hear if there was anyone about. Jenny let the hood of the jacket drop off the back of her head.

"Your ghost didn't draw this," she pointed out.

Billy motioned her to come and I walked behind them as slow as smoke might, though I was not even that substantial. I was melancholy and thinking in dreary metaphors. I was the moon by day, displaced and faded.

We followed Billy, watched him explore the stage right wings until he found what he was looking for. He grinned at Jenny and started up a built-in ladder beside the stage crew's work table, just as it appeared in the drawing. It was dark—Jenny came to the foot of the ladder and gazed up at the shape of Billy climbing into the blackness, ten, twenty feet up, then disappearing.

She had begun to ascend when his voice made her hurry.

"Wow."

I remembered the feeling of the hard wooden rungs through the soles of my shoes, but this time I floated up to the loft. When Jenny got to the top, Billy put a hand on the back of her head to make sure she didn't hit the slanted wooden beams. They had discovered the platform, no bigger than a bed, which would've been plain wood except for the thick black cloth that James and I had left there, a faded pile of curtain, spread across the surface. Jenny simply stared, but I dropped to the boards and wept.

The material was wrinkled, yet even in the low light it remembered the shape of two bodies.

CHAPTER 18

Jenny

I s that what I think it is?" asked Billy.

It was like we'd found an animal's den but the imprints left there were in the shape of two humans.

"How did you know this loft was here?" I asked him.

"Last year in carpentry we built a set for one of the plays."

Ever since Saturday night I had been almost remembering a dream I had about a boy who liked me — it was right on the edge of my brain. Every time I thought about it, I got that kind of joy rush like when I was little and woke up remembering we were leaving on vacation after breakfast. But it was also like the wave of nerves I got when I woke up remembering I had to give an oral report in history class that day. It wasn't the first time I'd dreamed I fell in love, but this dream was different.

In church the day before I thought I might have dreamed of a real boy, but one from the past. He might have been the spirit trying to make contact with me. I didn't want him to be dead or imaginary.

But now I was changing my idea about who had sent me messages in the pages of the Bible and about where that vision of a flood came from. Two spirits had been visiting my life, apparently, during my lost days, one in my body and one in Billy's. She was called Helen and I was starting to believe she was the one who guided my finger over the verses of Scripture.

I lay down on the cloth—Billy did the same, lying with his arm pressed to mine. We stared up into the jungle of ropes, lights, and electrical cords that hung above us, shifting almost imperceptibly in the blackness.

"I think Helen was trying to talk to me," I said. And I thought, *When she lay here with Billy's body, this is what she saw when she looked up.*

"How do you know it wasn't the male ghost?" Billy asked. "He was the one who fell in love with her in your body. Maybe he can't let go of you."

You would think this would be the answer—I dreamed of a ghost boy because Helen was in love with him and when he held her, the lips he kissed and the body he lay with was mine. You'd think I'd jump at the idea of my dream being a leftover memory of Helen's. But it didn't feel right at all.

The boy I dreamed about was on another planet, light-years away.

A voice from the stage below us made me jump. "Are these the only two things we have to paint?"

I grabbed Billy's hand.

"I think there's a table in the shop we're supposed to do, too," came another voice from twenty feet below us. "Or maybe a little desk."

I could hear the clink of a bucket handle, the shuffle of feet; I could smell paint.

Billy squeezed my hand.

"This can is half empty," said one boy.

"It's water-based, I think," said the other boy. "Maybe we could thin it out."

"We should go," I whispered to Billy, but he shushed me. A little too loudly.

"Shit!" said one of the boys below. "Did you hear that?"

I held my breath, frightened. Of what — being sent to the principal's office? Billy stifled a laugh.

"Hear what?" whispered the other boy. Then they both listened for a few moments while Billy and I stayed pressed together, trying to be still.

"This place is haunted," said the first boy.

"Really?"

"There's supposed to be a cold spot on stage."

"Weird." The second boy sniffed. "Hey, ghosts, don't bother us and we won't bother you."

Billy watched me, studying my face and throat, then held up a hand that said, *Don't worry, Miss, I'll take care of this.* He let out a long, low groan, just soft enough to be believable.

"Holy shit!"

Billy grinned as we heard paintbrushes clack to the floor and footsteps running away.

After a moment of silence, we climbed down. He took my hand as I stepped off the last rung — something about his treating me like a lady gave me a sudden jolt of pleasure. Here was a cute boy who liked me, and we had a secret story together — something no one else would ever guess at or understand. I knew my parents wouldn't let me date him, but he was my boyfriend anyway, I thought. I'd never had a boyfriend. I stared at him, amazed.

Billy adjusted his sweatshirt jacket on me, zipped me in, flipped the hood over my hair. I thought he was taking more time than he needed to.

"Am I disguised?" I asked. "Do I look like someone else?"

"Not to me," said Billy.

We waited until the bell rang for the next passing period and then slipped into the foot traffic, making our way back to the lockers. I saw Jill Sugden from church coming our way, so I ducked my head and pulled Billy in the other direction, toward the quad. Then out of the general crowd noise, someone behind us called out.

"Hey, Blake!"

This time it was Billy who changed our direction — he tugged me to the right, onto the path that led to the school office. I didn't want to be seen by anyone in attendance — they'd know I wasn't supposed to be at school today — but Billy was right. Whoever called out for him didn't follow us toward the principal's office.

We headed for the corner of the building where the bike racks were, but a teacher came out of the attendance office and almost ran into us. Mr. Brown paused to read one of those little phone message notes, and Billy and I stopped just in time. I had taken composition with him freshman year, and he was nice and sometimes funny, but it wasn't like I knew him very well. It took me a moment to remember that the ghost Helen said he had been her host. To my surprise, I was clutching his arm.

Mr. Brown looked down at me, expecting some student to ask

for a makeup quiz or to explain how they'd lost their book report, I suppose. His expression was open and relaxed, but when he saw my face in the shadow of the hood, he froze. He actually dropped his briefcase at his feet and the little note he'd been reading blew out of his fingers.

I was in shock, speechless. I wanted to let go of him, but it was like my hand belonged to somebody else. My shoulder felt heavy and tingling all the way down to my fingertips.

"I'm sorry," I blurted out.

Slowly he reached to put his hand over mine, but I was so embarrassed to be touching him that I tried to pull away. My hand wouldn't cooperate. In my clumsy struggle to free him I kicked his briefcase and a cardboard box slid out of it. My hand opened suddenly, letting go of him just as a gust of wind swept through the corridor and lifted the lid of the box on the ground and papers started blowing out of it.

We watched the pages blow around like birds. Then I had the irresistible urge to catch them. I ran at the papers, snatching them out of the air as they traveled past the bike racks and toward the parking lot. I reached and grabbed with my right hand and kept the captured ones in my left. I could hear Mr. Brown and Billy helping in the paper chase. Some of the pages were handwritten and some were typed, but as I lifted one from the ground and peeled another from where it stuck to someone's bicycle, I noticed that they weren't student homework. The handwriting was all alike and the typed pages had high numbers: 107, 113. It was all one manuscript. *His* manuscript, maybe. He carried it around hidden in a plain brown box in his briefcase.

I paused and looked at him. With hair ruffled in the wind and a mess of papers under one arm, he jumped up and caught another page in midair — he seemed like a kid, not like a teacher at all. He had a secret, like my photographs.

I dove at another page as it cartwheeled by my feet. I guessed the handwritten ones were especially important because these probably weren't entered into his computer yet.

Now Mr. Brown was ordering the papers in his hands and Billy was balancing on the bike rack to pull one from a tree branch. We gave our papers to Mr. Brown, who said, "Good work, team." He turned pages front-wise, right-side up, and flipped through, and as he started to order them by number he stopped and scanned the top one in puzzlement.

"Did we lose some?" I asked him.

"It doesn't matter," he muttered.

I felt guilty — I was the one who'd kicked his manuscript box open.

"I actually think this would make a better page one," said Mr. Brown.

"Did you write all that?" asked Billy.

Mr. Brown smiled, held his fat, wrinkled collection of pages to his chest, and gave a small bow. "To you, the patron saints of unpublished novels, many thanks."

If we'd had questions or apologies for each other, we didn't seem to anymore. We didn't even say goodbye. Billy took my hand, and as we walked away, Mr. Brown gave me a simple wave that lifted all the heaviness out of my arm.

We had to go back to the library because my mother would be wanting to pick me up. I hoped that if I called her before she got impatient and called *me*, she might let me study in the library again the
next day. Billy and I got muffins at the coffee house across the street
from the main branch and sat on the steps. I picked at mine, not
feeling hungry anymore.

"I have an idea for our next field trip," he said. "If I'm still
around."

"Are you going somewhere?" I asked. The idea that he might be
moving or going on vacation shook me up.

"Maybe," he said.

"Where?"

He looked into the distance and decided not to describe it. "Out
of town."

"For how long?" I asked.

This question seemed to pull all the energy out of him. "Don't
worry about it," he said.

A wave of fear swam up my spine as I saw something from the
corner of my eye that had often given me a stomachache — rolling
up to the curb, the white bulk of my father's van.

CHAPTER 19

Jenny

I RUMMAGED THE CELL PHONE out of my bag—I'd forgotten to turn the ringer back on after we'd left the library. I'd missed a call from home two minutes ago.

"What's wrong?" asked Billy.

"I have to go," I said. "Don't follow me." I started down the steps toward the van as the phone rang. My father parked in the no waiting zone as if rules didn't apply to him. He got out looking happy. He held a cell phone to his ear, a bright blue one I'd never seen before. The number on my mom's cell in my hand showed the word "Judy"—was he actually using his lover's cell phone to call me?

I didn't answer. I walked up to him and he hung up.

"What are you doing here?" I asked him.

"I needed to see you, Puppy."

"Mom's supposed to pick me up."

He sighed patiently. "Jennifer, I know you're angry with me right now, but get in the car. I'm not kidnapping you. Your mother knows I'm here."

I didn't want to throw a fit in front of Billy, who might still be watching us from the steps. As I opened the passenger door I realized I still had Billy's sweatshirt jacket tied around my waist. I slipped it off and stuffed it in my bag before sitting down in the front seat—my father didn't seem to notice.

He got behind the wheel and fastened his seat belt. My phone rang again, muffled by Billy's jacket pocket. I fished it out as we pulled away from the curb. It was home.

"Put on your seat belt," he ordered. "Just because your mother and I are ending our marriage does not mean I stop being your father."

I pulled the belt across my chest—it smelled like some flowery perfume, not like Mom. Then I answered the call.

"I'm okay, Mom."

"Your father is coming to get you." She sounded panicky.

"He's just bringing me home," I faced him. "Right, Daddy?"

He didn't bother to respond.

"He says he's not kidnapping me," I said. "See you in a few minutes." I put the phone into my bag. "You left without saying goodbye," I told him, but he didn't react at all. "Mom told me you're moving to San Diego."

"We are."

"What did you want to tell me?"

He raised one eyebrow but was in too good of a mood to actually be angry with me. "There's no need to be disrespectful."

He had always been the director of my tone. If he said I sounded belligerent or insincere or ungrateful, it was so. But this time instead of apologizing for sounding rude, I asked, "How long have you been seeing Judy?"

He gave a little puff of indignation, but smiled, pleased with himself. "That's none of your business, young lady."

He wore a shirt I'd seen him in dozens of times before, but he had the sleeves rolled up and he wasn't wearing his wedding ring. "We need to make plans," he said. He'd changed his hairstyle.

"If you're leaving, I should make plans with Mom from now on."

"Your mother does not decide what happens to you," he said. "You're still my daughter. I know what's best." We paused a little too long at a stop sign. I was afraid that he wasn't taking me straight to the house. That he would take me out to dinner or to Judy's place, but after a long moment he drove on toward home.

He was never frazzled, always right. I tried a different line.

"We didn't have as much time to get used to this as you," I reminded him.

Ignoring this, he said, "I hear your mother wants to homeschool you."

I pictured the pew where Judy always sat in church, right in front of us, and how she and my father often stood together talking at coffee hour.

"San Diego is beautiful," he said. These words made my stomach tense up. He'd been there with Judy already, I knew it. Some long weekend he'd pretended to be at a small business conference, probably. They'd chosen a neighborhood and maybe a house to rent.

I hated it when he got angry, but I couldn't stop the words that came out of me. "Does Judy have any children?"

His voice went cold. "You know she doesn't."

"Does she *want* kids?" I looked at him a long moment, and when he glanced over I knew he wasn't sure how to read my meaning. Was I asking if Judy wanted to have his babies? Or was I asking if she would be acting as my second mother?

"I didn't want to talk about it over the phone," he said. "I've decided it would be better for you to live with me in San Diego."

My ears started ringing.

"Your mother is simply an unfit parent. There's no way around it."

"What did Mom do?"

"Wives are responsible for the house and children." He was so relaxed, he rested his arm over the steering wheel, his wrist bouncing gently to some happy song I couldn't hear. He was wearing a new watch. Maybe Judy had bought it for him and he'd never been able to show it off until now. "Your mother was the one who let you get out of control." He wore a new, peppery aftershave like a teenager on a first date. "Let's face it," he sighed. "She's not smart enough to manage a budget, and she's ill-equipped to make money." He smiled at me sympathetically. "We both know what she's like," he said. "But no one knows her abilities and shortcomings better than I do."

I had an urge to slam my hand onto the steering wheel and lay into the horn, just to interrupt him. But I didn't, which made his sudden flinch a mystery. He swatted at a fly that wasn't there.

Recovering, he said, "You need guidance, and your mother's not spiritually mature enough to interpret God's plans for you. It's not her fault. Her character simply lacks the strength to protect you or manage your walk with Christ. I'm the one who has the means and the will to see you into adulthood."

There was no way even a man as cocky as my father could take me away from my own mother.

"You can pack a few of your things," he said. He was always so dismissive of my belongings. "But we'll buy you whatever you need. It'll be a fresh start."

My throat had tightened up. I suppose the silence bothered him.

"Don't you think it might be nice to begin again without people gossiping behind your back?" he asked me. "No one needs to know what happened here."

Before the car could come to a full stop outside our house, I opened my door and flung off my seat belt.

"I haven't finished," he reminded me.

I told him a lie I was sure would make him want to get away quick. "I think Pastor Bob is coming over in a few minutes."

That he drove off should have felt good, but he left a shadow over me that I couldn't escape. I tried to outrun it, but dread trailed after me as I ran up the walk and settled in deep as I found my mother in the dining room.

She had a dozen file folders and pieces of paper—receipts, letters, bank statements—spread across the table.

"He says we'll lose the house," she told me.

"Who says?"

"Your father's lawyer."

"That can't be true," I tried to tell her, but she was in another plane of reality.

"He won't sue for sole custody if I let you go to San Diego."

"No judge would give him that."

"More than fifty percent of cases find for the father."

"Did Daddy tell you that?" I put down my book bag and came to her side. "He lies."

"But people believe him." She started to cry, and I put my arm around her waist. I expected her to hold me, but she only held her eyes with one hand and a bank statement in the other. "I don't want to be alone," she sobbed. "They'll take you to church in San Diego and people will think she's your mother."

"I'm not going with him," I told her. "You're my only mom."

But as soon as I went to my room, I heard her go into the garage. I heard her drag the stepladder to the high shelves and the hollow scrape of her sliding down the big suitcases.

In my room I sat on the bed—I wanted someone to talk to but there was no one. Then I wondered about Helen. I scanned the room slowly in case she was nearby. *If she could send me messages in church, words, and visions of a flood*, I thought, *she might be in this room right now.* But I didn't know what to look for. She might look like a shadow or a mist or an orb of light. Or she might be completely invisible.

I jumped up and took my Bible from the dressing table. I stood in the middle of the room and held out the book. "Okay, Helen," I said aloud. "Talk to me." I dropped the Bible and it fell open. I picked it up without looking at the page and closed my eyes, slammed my finger down, but when I looked it had landed in the white space between columns.

I thought she might need to warm up. "Guide me," I said. I let my finger move all around both pages. I didn't feel any push or pull on my hand. I finally stopped and saw that my finger was pointing at a blank space again, this time between two chapters.

Maybe she was taking a vacation from me. Or maybe she didn't like to be ordered around. Or maybe she was done with earth and had moved on. I shut the Bible and set it aside.

Or maybe I had only imagined us having a conversation. I could have dreamed the flood because I was overwhelmed by everything. I was a bad soap opera.

I sat again on my bed. "Or maybe I'm just crazy," I said aloud. No ghost contradicted me.

But it felt like the mattress rocked very gently. Something light was sitting by my side.

CHAPTER 20

Jenny

This time Billy was already waiting for me just inside the library doors. Every time I saw him again I felt instantly happy: *I didn't imagine him—he is real.*

"Where are we going today?" I asked him as we walked to the bus stop. We'd already found the places his ghost had drawn—tree, phone booth, backstage in the auditorium, all but the inside of the school library.

"My house." He held my hand as if he was leading the way.

"Why?" I realized after I said the word that it sounded stupid.

"We know the ghosts went there together," said Billy. "In that picture of us, they were in my bed."

I was nervous—I liked him, more than he knew, but I didn't know what to expect. Did boys go around having sex with girls they hardly knew? Not the ones at church. At least I didn't think so. And we didn't remember being lovers. We were just getting to know each other.

We took the bus west, then transferred and went south a few blocks past the high school. On foot it only took a couple of minutes. Billy's house was small and old, with a scrawny tree in the front lawn. There were no cars parked outside, but still, after Billy took a key from the lip of the door frame and unlocked the house, he called, "Mitch?" And then, "Anybody?"

It seemed we were alone.

He motioned to me, put the key back, then closed the door, locking us in. I was startled by the living room. The furniture was beat-up and stained, magazines everywhere, a basket of unfolded laundry in front of the TV. It smelled like pine cleaner and wet newspapers.

When Billy swung the door of his room closed behind us, I couldn't help noticing the gash in it, as if someone had struck it with a baseball bat.

Maybe the photo of us proved that I *had* been here, but it didn't seem familiar. The narrow bed with a brown wool blanket, the bulletin board crammed with drawings, the posters and magazine pages corner to corner as if *Sports Illustrated* and *Rolling Stone* had been in the same recycle bin that then exploded all over the walls. I didn't remember any of it, but I liked the craziness.

Maybe he thought I was disgusted, because he said, "It's okay. We don't have to stay."

"It's nice," I said.

"Nice?"

"I mean, it's *you.*"

"Hey now," he said. "I don't have to take that kind of abuse."

"No, really," I told him. "It's the kind of room where you could just kick off your shoes and leave them in the middle of the floor instead of having to put them back in the shoe box and put the box on the shelf in your closet and close the closet and wipe your finger-prints off the closet door — "

"I believe you," he interrupted. "Feel free to kick off your shoes."

I pushed off my Keds, toe to heel. He sat on the desk chair and I sat on the bed, the one I didn't remember lying in naked.

On the board over his desk, one of the pinned-up sketches started to flap in a draft. It was the only one that wasn't a dragon or a monster. It was a beautiful line drawing of eyes. Maybe my eyes.

"I have something for you." Billy reached under the mattress, making the bed rock under me. He pulled out a piece of cardboard, the back of a tablet with all the pages used and torn off. It must not have been what he wanted, because he dropped it on the bed and reached under again.

I picked up the cardboard — one side was blank and the other had a long list of dates and numbers, *7/03 19 years, 6/08 6 weeks, 5/05 10 years*, etc. The list was titled: *C/PVS*.

"What's C slash PVS?" I asked.

Billy had a piece of notebook paper in his hand now and said, "Coma slash persistent vegetative state."

"Why?" I asked. "What are these dates?"

He took the cardboard from me and slid it back under the mattress. "Stories I found about people who wake up after doc-tors say they never will. It happens all the time." Billy unfolded the piece of paper, ready to present it to me, but I couldn't stop thinking about that list. The idea of him tracking miracles gave me a chill. It looked like he'd made a note of the dates they woke up and how long each person had been unconscious. His mother had been in a hospital and hadn't spoken a word in how many *years?*

"I think this was written for you." Billy smiled. He sat beside me on the bed.

I glanced over the single page of notebook paper he'd given me. "Is this a homework assignment?" I asked. It was labeled with Billy's name, September 16, English. I started to read it out loud. "The library smells like old books—a thousand leather doorways into other worlds."

"It's from when I was him," said Billy.

I kept reading. "I hear silence like the mind of God. I feel a presence in the empty chair beside me. The librarian watches me suspiciously. But the library is a sacred place, and I sit with the patron saint of readers. Pulsing goddess light moves through me . . ."

I stopped and Billy whispered, "I guess I should say, he wrote it for *her.*"

My heart took a shuddering surge forward. "Wow." Then I read, "Pulsing goddess light moves through me for one moment like a glimpse of eternity instantly forgotten. She is gone. I smell mold, I hear the clock ticking, I see an empty chair. Ask me now and I'll say this is just a place where you can't play music or eat. She's gone. The library sucks."

The soul who looked out of Billy's eyes in the photograph of us together had written this for the soul who had been looking out of me.

"And get this." Billy held the paper so we could look through it using the light from the window. "See?" He pointed out where the misspelled word *sacrid* had letters underneath that had been erased. "He misspelled a word on purpose."

I couldn't believe it. "Because he was pretending to be you?"

"Looks like it."

"Smart boy," I whispered. That the ghosts had to pretend to be us, the way I pretended to be what my parents wanted me to be, made me sorry for them. First you're alive, then you're dead, then you get a chance to be alive again and you have to walk around in disguise.

Billy stretched out on the bed. "Here's where that picture of us was taken." He examined the room from this position. I lay down beside him, my head next to his on the pillow — he put his arm behind his head to make room.

"Think of the stuff they probably talked about," he said. "How did you die? And why are you a ghost? Didn't heaven or hell want you?"

I rolled on my side to see if he was joking. "You think heaven wouldn't take them?"

"Well, how do you become a ghost?" He shrugged. "It's not like everyone who dies ends up like that."

That seemed sad, but at least they had each other. For a while. "I wonder when they first met," I said. "She was haunting Mr. Brown."

"I had Mr. Brown for English," said Billy. "So they were in the same classroom every day for fifty minutes."

He was lying on his side now, his head propped in one hand. A sheet of cold air came over me and I had a random thought that didn't seem like my own: *You have to step into a body if you want to smell grass again.*

"What's the matter?" he asked.

I closed my eyes and hid my face on his chest. As he put his arm around me, the wintry feeling lifted off my skin and I breathed in the heat coming through his shirt. I wasn't nervous anymore. I relaxed into him, safe and at home. I imagined we were lying under the stars, stretched out in a field of grass.

"I thought of a knock-knock joke," he said.

I must have heard him wrong.

"You know," he said. "Something you can't do alone."

I opened my eyes and used his arm as a pillow. "Okay."

"You really remember me from junior high?" he asked.

"I do."

"Will you remember me from now on?" he asked. "If you see me on the street someday, you won't pretend you don't know me?"

"I don't go around sharing amnesia ghost possessions with just anyone," I reassured him. "I will always remember you."

"Good." He sighed. "Knock knock."

"Who's there?"

"Billy."

"Billy who?"

"I told you you'd forget me."

I groaned. Sometimes he seemed like a twelve-year-old.

"Sorry," said Billy.

I laughed, but then I explained. "I'm not laughing at the joke. Do not take this as encouragement."

I jumped when the bedside table gave a shake. Nothing there

but a clock. It was already almost eleven. Billy narrowed his eyes and pointed his hand at it like Darth Vader trying to strangle the clock to death.

"What are you doing?" I asked.

"I'm trying to stop time."

CHAPTER 21

Jenny

IT WAS A SIMPLE, DORKY THING for him to say, but it felt like a comet went through my chest. *He stopped time for me.*

"There," he said. "Now we can lie here as long as we want."

He'd kissed me once before, when we were standing in my bedroom—a quick touch of the lips, but now he gave me a real kiss. My first. It should have been awkward, but it was like we'd been together forever. The room seemed to expand and the ceiling disappeared. I was loved and I was in a huge open field with all the air I could ever need.

I felt the seams of his shirt, turned wrong-side out, and the warm skin of his back as I slid my hand underneath. He pulled out of the kiss long enough to tug the shirt off, forward over his back and head. I could see the ceiling behind him, and the stars, too. I was afraid he would disappear, so I rose up and threw my arms around him so he wouldn't fly away. As we kissed he pulled the sleeves of my cardigan off one arm and then the other.

As long as we're touching, I thought, *wherever he goes, I'll go too, and wherever I go, I'll take him along.* It felt natural when he untucked my shirt from my pants so he could lay his palm flat on my stomach.

I thought someone was in the room. I turned my head to the side. He kissed my cheek, my temple, under my jaw, pressing me into the pillow. With my face turned to one side, I saw that there was someone beside me—too dim to see clearly, though. A boy on the grass, speaking, but I couldn't hear him. He sat up—he was trying to tell me something. I knew him, but I couldn't see him well enough.

"Wait." I gasped in a breath.

"Okay." Billy shifted his weight off me.

The room was back, the sky and the grass were gone—the ordinary daylight of autumn was almost blinding. I searched the ceiling and desk and clock. There was just me and Billy.

"This will sound crazy." I sat up and slid away from him.

"I doubt it," said Billy. "Compared to what?"

My throat tightened up—I didn't want to say anything about what I'd just seen. I didn't want it to sound like a dream, or a daydream, something I made up that means nothing. My eyes were hot—tears started down my face.

"Did I hurt you?" he asked.

I shook my head no. I was embarrassed to be crying in front of Billy.

"Are you scared? We don't have to do anything else."

"I'm not scared." My voice broke. "I was thinking about somebody . . ." I couldn't explain it.

Billy watched me, sitting on the side of the mattress. At first he held my hand. "Like who? Your parents?"

I shook my head, trying to dry my eyes with my bare hand.

"Like another guy?"

"Sort of."

His grip on my hand relaxed, his fingers slipped away. "A boy-friend."

"No," I said. "It's stupid. I don't even know his name or where he lives."

"A guy you like?" he asked. "From school?"

"No." I took a sharp breath, trying to suck my tears in and stop acting like an idiot. "It's ridiculous."

"I'm just not him," said Billy. "That's the problem, right?"

"No," I told him. "There's nothing wrong with you."

"But you can't stop thinking of him when you're with me?"

I wanted to climb onto the roof and hide.

"I get it." Billy stood up and grabbed his shirt from the floor. He pulled it on, right-side out this time. It had a picture of a zombie on it. He sat on his desk chair.

"I think I met someone during the time I had amnesia," I told him.

Billy studied me for a long moment. "It's him, the ghost who was in my body."

I'd wondered that before, but no, it still didn't sound right. "I don't think so."

"You're remembering him, that's why you can't think of his name."

I shook my head. "When I left my body I didn't go to school or here," I said. "I was far away. Where there was lots of sky and air." It sounded so childish, but that's the best way I could describe it, because it was just on the outside edge of my memory.

Billy stared me—all the color had faded out of him.

"Our bodies were here, but our spirits weren't," I told him. "Where did *your* spirit go?"

He shrugged. "Maybe my spirit was asleep." Then he picked up my sweater and held it out to me. "I'll take you back to the library. If you want me to."

It felt like he was kicking me out. "I'm sorry," I said. "I didn't mean to hurt your feelings. Forget everything I said."

"It's okay. I get the idea." He was still holding out the sweater, so I took it. "I'm not mad," he told me.

I pulled the sweater on and looked around for my shoes, but I knew I should say something else.

"It's not like we're in love," he told me, but the more he talked, the less he sounded okay. "People I love end up in the hospital or jail. Better to stay clear of the curse."

"Don't be stupid," I said. "You're not cursed." Even though I had been feeling like there was someone else and that kissing Billy was sort of like cheating, the idea that Billy wasn't in love with me and that he didn't want to be my boyfriend anymore made me feel sick to my stomach.

"Here." He put my shoes into my hands in a rough way that made me stare at him. Looking embarrassed, he backed away a step, bumped into his desk, and leaned against it. "Sorry." He sighed. "Take your time."

As I was putting on my shoes the bedside table shook again and another gust of cool air rushed at me—I could feel the pressure of icy fingers gripping my arm, pulling me to my feet.

But Billy wasn't touching me.

"What is it?" he asked.

Then we both heard a car door slam. I ran into the hall, hoping I could act as if Billy and I were visiting in the living room instead of his bedroom. The front door opened just as I was struggling to get my heel into my second shoe, balanced on one foot in the entryway. Billy set my book bag down next to me as Mitch looked from one of us to the other.

"What did I tell you?" Mitch slammed the door.

"She's just leaving," said Billy. "Don't worry. She dumped me."

I stood up and realized my shirt was not tucked in, but I was too shy to fix it in front of his brother.

Mitch looked me up and down, and even though his fists were tight, his face relaxed as he picked up my bag. "Time to go," he told me.

I hoped Billy would try to stop us, or at least come with us, but he sat on the arm of the couch looking exhausted as Mitch led me out on the porch.

I wanted to go back and tell him that I loved him, even if he didn't feel the same. I opened my mouth but no words came out. *I can tell him at school,* I thought. Only we would never go to the same school again. I panicked at the idea of losing him. With the ghosts gone, there was nothing linking the two of us anymore. If he didn't want me, I was lost.

Mitch shut the door and was leading me down the steps by the elbow as if I might run for it. I asked him to take me to the library and he gave me a funny look.

"My mother's picking me up there," I explained.

He smiled at the idea that I had lied to her about my plans for the day. On the way there he held an unlit cigarette in his mouth for a while, finally flicking it to the dashboard when there were only a few blocks to go.

"Did you really break up with him?" he asked.

"I guess," I told him. "I'm not sure what happened."

Mitch didn't look at me—kept his gaze on the road and the rearview mirror. "He's a good kid, but he doesn't need another heartbreak right now."

I didn't know what to say. I wanted Billy. Maybe I didn't deserve him, but it was too sad how short a time together we'd had.

"I know you'll probably change your mind in a few hours," said Mitch. "I'm not blind. I can see how you are together, but we don't even know what's happening to him after tomorrow."

"What's tomorrow?" I asked.

"Did he really not talk about any of that?" Mitch sighed. He reached up and caught the cigarette again as he pulled up to the curb outside the main branch. He put the car in park and took a lighter from his pocket, waiting for me to get out before he lit up.

"Is Billy in trouble?" I asked as I opened my door.

Mitch paused with the flame ready. "Nothing for you to worry about, kid. Have a nice life."

A puff of smoke trailed after the car as it drove off.

CHAPTER 22

Helen

ALL THE WAY HOME FROM THE LIBRARY, Cathy was lost in thought. She didn't notice that Jenny was sad. At home, the dining room table was stacked high with organized file folders, photocopied papers stapled or paper-clipped together; accordion files with titles such as HOUSE and MONTHLY EXPENSES stood beside open file boxes.

Jenny reached to open a file labeled PARENTING but withdrew her hand when Cathy came into the room.

"Dad was the one who left us," Jenny told her. "He can't get custody of me."

"He says legally—"

Jenny interrupted her. "He doesn't know how the law works."

"He knows how to make deals," said Cathy. "He knows how to blackmail people."

"But you won't let him take me." Jenny came up and stood beside Cathy's shoulder. "Right?"

Cathy was looking over her documents, eyes flicking nervously from one to another.

"I'm trying," she said absently.

"You're my mom," said Jenny.

I wanted to sweep her away from rejection, but she needed to ask her mother for help. She needed to see with her own eyes, and hear for herself, if Cathy was not up to the task of loving her.

"Don't I get to say who I want to go with?" Jenny asked.

Cathy put a belated arm around the girl's shoulder. A hollow gesture, not even an afterthought. "I didn't get your homeschooling materials yet," she said. "I can go tomorrow."

"It's okay." Jenny rested her head on Cathy's shoulder. "Mom?"

She answered automatically. "Yes?"

"You know during the time I can't remember . . . Did my voice sound different?" Jenny looked up at her mother, waiting. "Did I use words I don't usually use, or did I have an accent or anything?"

"What?" Cathy separated from the girl, her brow tight and strained. "Of course not. Why?"

"Not even the last few days before I went to the hospital?" Jenny seemed oblivious to Cathy's fear, but I could feel it like a grating vibration in my teeth. "I didn't talk funny?" Jenny asked.

Cathy took another step back. "Funny in what way?"

Jenny shrugged. "Old-fashioned, maybe?"

Cathy grew pale and walked into the living room. "Don't be ridiculous."

Jenny followed her, watched her mother straighten things that were already neat. "I'm trying to figure out what happened to me," said Jenny. "Weren't there moments when I seemed like someone else?"

I remembered vividly the conversation Cathy and I had after her women's group meeting. We stood on the sidewalk in the dark and I told her I wasn't her daughter. Cathy had been in tears. Even now I could almost hear the sprinklers in a stranger's yard and smell the wet pavement. And Cathy recalled it too—I could see it in the lines around her eyes and where a smile should have been.

Cathy moved to the open arch of the hall doorway, keeping her back away from her daughter. "I don't like this," she told Jenny.

"Do you believe spirits can visit us and take over our bodies?"

"Spirits?" Cathy folded her arms. "What kind of spirits?"

"I don't know." Jenny came a step closer to her mother and Cathy tensed.

Coward, I said. *Talk to her. She's your only child. Her father will never explain anything to her.*

"You and Daddy always had answers about stuff like this," said Jenny. "Angels and visions and the Holy Ghost. That's why I'm asking. Do you think a spirit was visiting me?"

"Are you talking about an angel?" asked Cathy.

Jenny hesitated. Too long for Cathy's comfort. "I don't think so."

Cathy's voice turned hard. "I don't want to talk about this anymore." She marched down the hall and at first Jenny followed.

In the corridor Cathy turned on every light she came to. The hall was lit. The overhead light as she walked into her bedroom, the end table lamp. Even the TV across from the bed.

She grabbed the remote, turned on the television, then pressed the volume control until a row of little blue bars grew across the bottom of the screen and the blare of the weather channel surrounded her with a protective wall of noise. For an extra measure, she closed the bedroom door against any conversations about the supernatural.

Jenny stayed in the hall long enough to take two breaths, then went into her own room and closed us in. She sat at her dressing

table and stared first at her own face, then at the closet doors behind her in the reflection. The mirrored surface on the doors would
normally send her a view of her own back and of her face in the
vanity's glass, but the closet was half opened, the mirror not showing.

I moved into her line of sight. Something in the backwards
reflection, in the space where I stood, captured her attention. She
drew a tissue from the box on her dressing table, leaned forward,
and rubbed at the glass — I wondered if she could see some vague
form of my specter and mistook it for a smudge.

Feeling bold, I glided in front of her, facing the reflection, and
lowered myself until my eyes lined up with hers. She was seeing
herself *through me*. I didn't mean to scare her — I wanted to be
acknowledged — but she must have seen some wisp of me, for she
drew in her breath and lurched back from the table.

She darted to the door and I thought she would flee the room,
but instead her gaze fell to the library books on the desk next to
her, the ones that used to be in her school bag. She snatched up
the top one from the stack, *Jane Eyre,* and sat down on the floor
right where she was. After one unsteady breath, she let the book fall
open across her knees. I had been frustrated the night before by my
sometimes successful, often failed attempts to speak to her through
the printed word, but I decided to try again.

I had taken control of her hand to touch Mr. Brown when we
came upon him in the high school hallway. But that was a frightening, awkward ordeal. I tried to remember how I had taken gentle
control of James's hand when we wrote together at the back of Mr.
Brown's classroom. I had relaxed him. So now I rested my hand on
Jenny's back, then I slid my palm down her arm from shoulder to

wrist. She shuddered for a moment, then let me move her hand, my fingers wrapped around hers, pointing her index finger where I willed it.

I scanned the page and quickly chose a phrase I hoped would express my difficulty in communicating with Jenny: *I could not very well understand her.*

Jenny gasped, but did not pull away from my influence. She whispered, "More."

I helped her turn several pages and chose the line: *my eyes sought Helen.*

"Helen," she whispered, her voice thinned with awe. "Why did you take my body?"

I went ahead to another page, chose another phrase: *I must love him.*

"Why did you *leave* my body?" she asked.

I folded over a few chapters of the book and from the page I found I pointed to the words *something not right.*

"Why are you still here?" she wanted to know.

I turned a few pages farther along: *to comfort you, as well as I could.*

Then I skipped forward several more pages and showed her: *I am here; and it is my intention to stay till I see how you get on.*

In a jarring trill, the phone rang, the sound rolling through the halls. I couldn't remember how many phones Jenny's family had. Three? Four? They all cried at once.

The spell was apparently broken. Jenny listened toward the hall for a moment—the sound stopped in the middle of the second ring—and Jenny put her hand into the book again, but she wouldn't let me control her now. She sighed and left the book on the floor. She went to the bed and lay on her side, scanned the room, then asked, "Are you still here?"

I tried speaking the word, but she couldn't hear me, even when I shouted it. I tried flickering the lamp, then moving the curtain, but nothing worked. Finally I sat beside her and tapped her shoulder. Nothing. I tapped the back of her hand and she jumped.

She looked frightened at first, but then she lay her hand on the bedspread palm down, offering it to me. I drew a *Y* for the word *yes* on her skin and she shivered.

"Yes?" she asked. I wrote the *Y* again.

"Is your name Mary?" she asked with half a smile.

I wrote an *N* for "no." She gave a small sound of surprise.

"Is your name Helen?" she asked.

I drew the *Y* again. Jenny closed her eyes for a moment and took a slow breath, in and out, before asking, "Are you an angel?"

I indicated that no, I was not.

Jenny's smile dropped. "You aren't evil, are you?"

Well, I was not without sin — I wasn't sure how to answer. Finally I told her no.

"A ghost?" she asked.

Yes — I told her twice.

To test me again, I suppose, she asked, "Your name is Sarah, right?"

No, I indicated, and then along her arm I wrote with my finger in block letters as if I were a child practicing at a chalkboard: H E L E N. Jenny shuddered again and let out a breath as if she was chilled.

"Wow," she whispered. "Helen is here to comfort me."

Y for *yes.*

"Did you drown?"

Yes.

Perhaps my finger was cold on her skin, for she pulled the covers over her legs and wrapped her free arm around her waist. The other stayed on the bed, waiting for my answers.

"Why do you care how I feel?" she asked. "My father doesn't — he hates me. I don't even think my mother likes me very much."

Silly girl, I said aloud, but she couldn't hear me. *Of course I care for you.*

"And Billy used to like me," she said. "But I ruined that."

I wrote on the back of her hand: *N.*

"I did," she insisted. "I don't think he wants to see me again. I hurt his feelings."

I was about to draw a heart on the back of her hand, but she asked another question: "Where is your sweetheart?"

Up her arm I spelled *heaven.*

"He must miss you," she said, which froze me for a moment. How awful if he was missing me, but how much worse if he was not. Could she have sensed my worry? She drew a *Y* for *yes* on the back of her own hand as she said, "Yes, he does."

Then she sat up with a new idea. "Do you know about a boy I met when I was away from my body?"

She held her hand out in midair and I wrote, *N* for *no.* I had no way of knowing what people, ghosts, angels, or other kinds of creatures she might have visited.

She nodded, trying not to look disappointed. "Maybe I dreamed him." She lay back down and thought for a moment while I sat on the corner of the mattress. Finally she said, "There's no one else to talk to. Will you talk to me?"

Yes, I told her.

"If I have a nightmare, will you come to me?"

Yes.

"If I can't go back to sleep, will you stay with me?"

Yes, yes.

"If I'm lost and I call you, will you come help me?"

Yes. I wrote on her arm, *Love.*

"Billy doesn't like me anymore," she repeated. Tears rose in her eyes.

No, I told her, but gently she shook her head.

"He told me to leave," said Jenny. "I didn't even say goodbye."

I lay my palm on the top of her head and to my surprise, she fell asleep, with the blankets folded across her legs and her pale hand spread out on the bed.

When I had first become Jenny I had been terrified by the sound, but now the rushing water no longer reminded me of death. The shower shut off, Jenny toweled herself dry and rubbed her hair until it stopped dripping. I wondered if she had forgotten about me — she hadn't addressed me since her nap. All through dinner and the doing of dishes, nothing indicated she was listening for me or wondering where I was. Now she slipped her nightgown over her head, brushed her teeth. I wished I could help her comb out her hair, as I had with my own girl on my knee, but my hand went through the brush.

Jenny chose a comb instead and began to untangle her wet hair. When she paused, I did not know what she was thinking. She didn't

seem alarmed in any way, and neither did she speak to me. She matter-of-factly drew a tampon from a box under the sink. At first this
seemed mundane—I had lived with my last host and his wife for
long enough to find the concept ordinary. But when Jenny had applied it and dropped the wrappings in the trash basket, she dropped
a tissue into the toilet—before it was flushed away I caught sight
of blood.

Pain weighty as a brick fell through me. I remembered now that
when James and I were in Billy's and Jenny's bodies we might have
created a child. Of course I would not have wanted Jenny to con-
ceive out of wedlock and at such a young age, but I caught myself
on the edge of the tub and wept. Jenny stood again at the bathroom
mirror, staring at herself until the comb clattered into the basin.
She clutched the counter and began to shake—she lowered herself
onto the floor near me as the tears came.

CHAPTER 23

Helen

I WANTED TO REACH FOR HER, but I was too weak.

Almost at once Cathy was in the doorway, gaping at her daughter. Jenny's cries were hoarse and childlike—her sobs rattled in my own chest.

"What happened?" Cathy demanded.

Jenny couldn't speak at first. Cathy lowered the lid of the toilet and helped her to sit there. Finally Jenny spoke.

"I'm bleeding."

"Where?"

"My period," she told her.

The girl was grieving. But Cathy didn't embrace her. So I knelt beside Jenny and wrapped my arms around her. We wept together while Cathy hovered, practically twitching with nerves.

"What's sad about that?" asked Cathy.

"I lost the baby," Jenny cried.

I know, I whispered.

"What?" Cathy made an exasperated click of her tongue.

"It's gone and they'll never be back," said Jenny.

It's not your fault, I said. *Hush now.*

"What baby?" Cathy asked. "*Who* will never be back?"

"I'm sorry," Jenny told me. She held her stomach as I stroked her hair.

Cathy's tone was stern. "Jennifer Ann, you were not pregnant."

"I don't know if it was a boy or a girl," Jenny sobbed.

It was a little girl, I told her.

"That's absurd." Cathy stormed out of the room. How shocking to desert her child that way.

I leaned my head against Jenny's and rocked her. *There's nothing to be done,* I told her, and I meant to be comforting, but I couldn't help imagining what it would have been like if my baby girl had died when she was a newborn. I saw her tiny head in the cradle, her rose-gold fuzzy hair when she was only a few days old — I imagined her skin snow white and my hand lowering to her cheek and finding it ice-cold.

I gasped at the idea. Jenny cried out as if she had been struck, and the tears flowed anew.

Cathy stomped back into the bathroom as if the girl's grief were a personal insult. She had something in her hand. "Look, your period is supposed to start now. See?"

It was the chart from Jenny's desk, the calendar marked with a red dot on each day that Jenny had her period and a red circle when it would probably start the next month. Jenny gulped in air and blinked at the red circle on tomorrow's date.

"Now can we stop this nonsense?" asked Cathy.

"I know she was a real baby," Jenny said.

She was, I whispered, angry at Cathy for being so dismissive. Of course she was real. I could see the baby's lopsided grin and feel her chubby fingers clutching at my clothes and hair.

"I was supposed to keep her safe," Jenny insisted.

"Her?" Cathy felt Jenny's forehead for fever, but she did it with such a lack of sympathy that I tried to swat the woman's hand away. "There is no *her*," Cathy sighed.

"She would have looked like him," Jenny cried.

My heart ached at this. She would have looked like James, this baby girl who was not to be.

"Heaven forbid," Cathy whispered. Jenny didn't seem to hear, but I flew up and tried to shove Cathy out of the room. The woman jumped as if a bee had flown in her face. She searched the air but could not see who or what had attacked her, I supposed.

"Honestly, Jennifer," said her mother. "Do you think the doctors would miss something like that when they examined you and did all those tests?"

These words gave me pause. As soon as I let go of Jenny, the girl took in a long breath. The tears stopped.

"You don't want to have that boy's baby, do you?" Cathy asked.

Jenny blinked and rubbed her eyes dry with her nightgown sleeves. I was taken aback by how suddenly she'd stopped crying. The idea struck me that Jenny had never been pregnant. It was only a thought, a possibility that came to me just before I left her body.

"Well?" Cathy demanded.

"No." Jenny looked dazed. I knelt beside her and took her hand.

"There was no baby," I whispered, but the loss caught in my throat.

Immediately Jenny's tears were back, rolling down her cheeks. I let go of her and jumped away.

They were my tears.

"You did not have a miscarriage." Cathy held a box toward her and Jenny pulled out a tissue, rubbed her eyes and face.

"Okay," she told her mother. "I get it."

My baby, I whispered. To see if I was right. Jenny's chin began to tremble and she pressed the tissue to her eyes.

I was the cause of her grief. My sorrow was making her ill. My Jenny, whom I would fight demons to protect, I was haunting her. Being so long away from heaven had clouded my thinking. I tried to shift my thoughts to something that wouldn't grieve her so, but I could only think of how I was darkening her spirit and how I might lose her and how I had no one on earth but her.

She sobbed into her hands.

I took a step back from her and she pulled in a deep breath. I took another step away and she dried her cheeks and tossed the tissue into the trash basket. I backed away into the bathroom wall, and Jenny's voice sounded stronger and brighter.

"I'm okay," she told Cathy. "I don't know what I was thinking."

My heart shrank as I stepped backwards into the dark, through the wall of the house, into the still night garden, away from my girl.

The backyard was as far as I went at first. I hid against the garden wall. I knew I would have to leave her—it was clear I was hurting her. The worst part was that I had no idea what damage had already been done. I wanted to be safe and fly far away, but something about it still felt like a sin. I was abandoning her.

I worried my hands together, which strangely seemed to create a small cloud of mist to form around me, sparkling the bricks with dew. I couldn't leave her a note and was afraid any message I might try to send through words or thoughts might upset her. So at last I resolved to go back the way I'd come.

Having scaled this mountain before, you'd think I would find it easier to climb the second time, but I couldn't see how it worked. Heaven felt to me now as far away as Wonderland or Oz — I believed, but I had no map. No key. I felt there was some trick to do with the horizon folding like a piece of paper, but I was muddled again.

The lights in the house were all dark now. But as I began to worry that I would never find my way to heaven, I saw Jenny's bedroom lamp come on. She couldn't sleep. My fault, no doubt. I was ashamed. I couldn't help myself — I floated to a place along the garden wall where I could see into her bedroom window. She sat in bed, looking around the room, holding the back of her hand up for me to send her a message.

But I couldn't risk bringing her pain that was not her own. Without a plan I began to run through the wall in her backyard and into the next yard and the next, through fence and hedge and over the silver surface of swimming pools.

I tried to remember the moment I'd climbed into heaven when I left her the first time, but there was a darkness in the place of that memory like a night sky where stars refuse to gather. I stopped running and found myself in the driveway of a stranger's yard, the light from their kitchen window tilting down into the grass.

If I couldn't recall how I'd entered heaven the first time, I'd have to retrace my steps from my arrival in Jenny's life the second time. I'd left James in heaven and come back to Jenny. There was a path there, there must have been.

When I tried to imagine heaven and being there with James, images came to me so vague and small, I hardly believed them. There was a table under a tree and someone played piano. Could I have actually left him by simply slipping my fingers out of his grasp and turning away, stepping down a staircase, or perhaps the slope of a hill? I moved toward a place where the shadow of the path ahead and the trees on either side became one darkness.

Now I began to walk forward through this stranger's yard and felt distinctly as if I was moving farther and farther from my destination. So, like a fool, I stopped and placed my right foot back behind me, then my left, walking slowly backwards toward what I hoped was heaven.

I closed my eyes, since I was not using them to guide me. The harder I tried to remember how to get back, the more the idea became confused. A shadow, a blank wall, an empty road. I would briefly, every so often, forget what I was trying to concentrate on. Finally all I was left with was the peculiar idea that when I came to earth and landed beside Jenny's bathtub, what lay ahead of me just before I slid back to earth had become still, like a scene from toile de Jouy wallpaper, thin and then unreadable, as if I was passing out of the room and the wall was shortening. The picture became darker and narrower and eventually unrecognizable.

That's what had happened, wasn't it? I found the thin place in the curtain between heaven and earth by moving toward the tilting, narrowing focal point on the shadowed horizon. That's when I slipped through the slit like a letter, as fragile as a pressed flower.

I wasn't walking anymore, I was running blindly backwards, causing spider webs to tremble and owls to startle and flutter to other branches. Crickets hushed as I rushed by. Though invisible, I set off a motion light in one backyard, and while I crossed a street a plastic bag swooped up after me, drawn by my anxiety rather than my disturbing the actual air.

But by and by my lack of direction curled my path into a circle and I slowly spun to a stop in an empty lot crisp with dead weeds and dry grass. I feared that my failing to protect Jenny, my abandoning her, was keeping me from finding my way. I shook with horror — I tried to steel myself with anger.

"It's not fair!" I shouted.

My voice rang around me, vexing me with echoes. I curled in on myself and huddled on the ground. I tried to comfort myself by picturing James or the sweet face of my daughter, but they were clouded. I couldn't recall the needle-eye slit of heaven, but now in my wretchedness I remembered the other place.

It didn't take anything more than that, just the admission that I could remember hell. The space was small, only a little larger than a coffin, really. The water was higher now, nearly to the ceiling. It tasted of metal and earth and an odd mix of plant spices, a recipe made by nature in a wild tantrum. Sage, mint, and honeysuckle, but also anise, parsnip, and the bitter bloom of chrysanthemum.

Above the cellar door, as seen through a gap where a tree limb had torn through, lightning flashed, sending a moment of blue-green brightness into the water. The storm danced outside to its perverse music — the familiar din of thunder cracks, the hiss of rain, and that singular howl that always sickened me.

It used to be that my hell was alive and screaming, winds blowing, water spraying, thunder and lightning in full flash and roar. Now, though, it stopped, still and mute. The cold was there, though — I could feel the chill deep in my soul. Perhaps this pause in my hell was worse than its past torment. Movement might imply the possibility of an end someday. But this stillness was unbearable.

Perhaps it wasn't that time had frozen but that it was now moving at the pace of infinity. A moment now becomes a century.

I could see through the dark pool two pale shapes, my hands, like drowned doves floating just under the surface two feet before me. Tickling at my scalp, a crown of water, for I had been swallowed up.

CHAPTER 24

Jenny

I COULDN'T BELIEVE MY MOTHER WANTED me to go to the library. Billy wouldn't be there. I had no reason to go anymore. But she gave me lunch money and her phone.

"Some of the women from church are coming over," she explained.

I assumed they would be talking about my father. "I could stay in my room," I told her.

But she dropped me off at the usual stop and all she said about it was "I'll call when I'm ready to get you."

I climbed the steps to the entrance as slowly as if my veins were filled with lead. Helen had left me. I waited until after midnight for her to speak to me, but she never answered. Not this morning, either. Maybe she was done watching over me. Maybe I was crazy and had just imagined her. Nothing would surprise me anymore.

And Billy had had enough of me too. He'd told his brother that I'd broken up with him, but it didn't feel like that to me. I wanted to see him again—I hadn't said goodbye. So I stood on the steps to get decent reception and used my mother's phone.

Instead of hello, a man answered saying, "Mitch?"

The voice didn't sound like Billy or his brother.

"No," I said. "It's Billy's friend."

"Yeah?" He waited.

Mitch had said something was going to happen to Billy today. I had nothing to lose—I started lying. "I was supposed to go with them," I said. "Am I too late?"

"They left half an hour ago."

"Yeah," I said. "I thought so. Can you give me the address? I'll meet him there."

"It's the Prescott building, the one downtown that looks like a resort, with the palm trees."

After hanging up I went inside the library long enough to find out where the Prescott was and which bus would take me there.

It was a three-story building covered in blue mosaics. I walked in and read the directory by the elevator. I had no idea where Billy was or what he was doing in this kind of place—most of the offices belonged to lawyers. I couldn't hear Billy's voice, or any voices, but I started walking down every hallway listening. As I came up to conference room number nine on the first floor and looked through the window in the door, I saw Billy. He wore a blue pullover sweater and sat in a wooden chair in front of a long table. The room was huge—they were only using one end. Billy looked tired but sat straight, his sneakers planted firmly on the floor. He wasn't facing the door, so he didn't see me spying on him.

A woman and a man, both wearing dark suits, sat at the table taking notes, though there was a microphone and a recorder doing the same thing. Four people were sitting in folding chairs near the table: Mitch and an older woman and a middle-aged couple. They sat several seats apart as if they didn't know each other.

The woman at the table had a cardboard nameplate that read MS. IVERS and the man's plate read MR. SAWYER. At the far end of the table, a man in a light blue suit sat behind a nameplate labeled A.D.A. FARMINGTON, and next to him was a bald man with a tripod and camcorder aimed at Billy.

Mitch hung his head, playing with a piece a nicotine gum in its domed packaging.

A security guard walked up to me from down the corridor. "That's a private deposition."

"I'm family," I lied to him.

He motioned me to be quiet, led me to a second door at the far end of the room, and silently pushed the door open just enough for me to slip in. I found a folding chair against the wall just inside and sat. No one noticed me. I held myself perfectly still, trying to blend in with the wall. I'd come to talk to Billy, but I'd have to wait—he seemed to be giving a statement. From my seat I could watch Billy in profile.

Ms. Ivers played with her pen as she spoke. "Mr. Blake, did the district attorney offer you probation instead of incarceration in this case?"

"Yeah." Billy picked at the threads of a tiny hole that was starting in the knee of his jeans.

"Why?"

Billy glanced at Mr. Sawyer. "They wanted me to testify against Grady and Roth."

"That implies my clients are guilty and you're innocent," said Ms. Ivers. "But weren't you an integral part of this crime?"

"I don't know about integral," said Billy. "But I don't think I'm innocent."

Mr. Sawyer shifted but didn't speak. Mitch looked like he was about to get up and shake some sense into his brother.

Ms. Ivers leaned forward. "You're not innocent? What are you guilty of?"

"I should have stopped it," said Billy.

"You could have been the hero?" she asked.

"I just mean, I think I could have stopped it if I tried." Billy thought for a second. "I'm sure I could have."

"Didn't Miss Dodd make a statement that you were an eyewitness to the assault?"

"That's incorrect," Mr. Sawyer interrupted. "Miss Dodd amended her statement."

"Yes, I'm sorry," said Ms. Ivers. "Miss Dodd later says that it was Mr. Roth who observed." Ms. Ivers made a note on her legal pad. "But she recognized you. Seeing you on campus at your high school was how she was able to track down Mr. Grady and Mr. Roth, isn't that right?"

"Yeah," said Billy. "She probably remembered me because I was the first one to talk to her."

Ms. Ivers made another note. "Isn't it true you have a memory gap of over two weeks in length?"

Billy seemed to sense a trick. "Yeah."

"Isn't it true that when first arrested you claimed you could not testify against my clients because you didn't remember the event?"

Billy nodded.

Mr. Farmington said, "Please speak your response."

Billy cleared his throat and sat up straighter. "That's what I was told. Yeah."

"That's what you were told?" Ms. Ivers asked. "Meaning you don't recall making that statement?"

"Right."

"So you do in fact remember the crime in this case."

"Yeah."

Ms. Ivers twirled the pen in her fingers. "Six days ago you visited your father, who is in prison, correct? That's when you changed your story?"

Billy glanced at Mr. Sawyer, who said nothing. "The story never changed. I just couldn't remember what happened until that day."

"Was it getting a glimpse of prison life that made you suddenly remember what supposedly happened, that it was my clients alone who committed the rape?"

The word hit me so hard I couldn't breathe. The room seemed to tilt — my stomach shifted. Maybe I hadn't heard right.

"I'm telling the truth," Billy said. "Give me a lie detector test if you want."

"Just answer all questions honestly," said Mr. Farmington. "And remember that you're under oath."

My body was rebelling — the instinct was to run. My legs, acting on their own, started to tense as if I was about to stand up. Now I was breathing too fast — my vision started to go salt-and-pepper. I thought of putting my head down so I wouldn't faint, but I didn't want to look away from Billy.

"The truth is, I have this gap in my memory," he said. "So I don't remember driving to the prison or walking in. I sort of woke up in the visiting room and my dad was sitting there at a table and he looked really old. Anyway, Mitch was yelling at him and crying—" Billy stopped as if he'd told too much. "I could remember everything then, except the two or three weeks before."

"You said you 'woke up'?" asked Ms. Ivers. "Were you sleep-walking?"

"No."

"Was it an alcohol- or drug-induced blackout?"

"I don't think so."

Mr. Sawyer cut in. "My client is not qualified to answer that question."

"Were you intoxicated or high on the day of the crime?" asked Ms. Ivers.

"No," said Billy.

"How about now?" she asked. "Did you take anything today?"

Billy sighed, his patience getting thin. "No." He glanced at the ADA. "Can I just tell you what happened?"

"I advise my client to only answer the questions put to him," said Mr. Sawyer.

"I want to make a statement," said Billy. "That's not against the law, is it?"

Ms. Ivers leaned back in her chair smugly.

"My lawyer didn't tell me to keep anything from you. He said I should say only what's necessary. And keep it short," said Billy. "Maybe it would be better for me if I kept it short, except this thing is hard to explain. I'm going to tell you exactly what happened to me, even if it sounds crazy."

"Jesus," Mitch sighed.

"I couldn't sleep after." Billy stopped for one second, choosing his words. "I couldn't sleep after the crime, and it hurt to think about it, so I tried different things to stop thinking. I started piling stuff on top of each other until I passed out."

"What do you mean by 'stuff'?" asked Ms. Ivers.

"Xanax, pot, glue." Billy went back to pulling the threads on the knee of his jeans. "I remember lying there and I couldn't move. But then I felt like I got free from my body. Like flying away. And when I came back into my body"—he shrugged—"it was weeks later." Billy forced himself to leave the worn spot on his jeans alone and folded his arms. "That's why I can remember the crime perfectly but not those days I was away. During those weeks I think someone else was living in my body."

Ms. Ivers's pen stopped twirling. "Someone else was in your body?"

"Yeah, I think so," said Billy. "That was him that said he couldn't testify because he didn't remember the crime. And that's why I didn't remember making that statement."

She held perfectly still. "Is this someone an alternate personality?"

"My client is not qualified to answer that question," said Mr. Sawyer.

Ms. Ivers made some quick notes on her pad. "You used the word 'crazy,'" she said. "Is your lawyer planning to use any of this 'out of body' testimony as part of a diminished capacity defense in case your deal with the DA falls through?"

"My client—" Mr. Sawyer started, but Ms. Ivers waved away his objection.

"The question is withdrawn."

"I may not be the smartest guy in the world, and I may not be innocent, but I don't think I'm crazy," said Billy.

Mitch sat crackling his nicotine gum wrapper.

Ms. Ivers smiled at Billy, pleased, as if she sensed a weakness she could take advantage of. "So you say you didn't know what my clients, these two friends of yours, were going to do on the day of the crime, yet you've admitted that you've stolen things with them, you've vandalized street signs and a park fountain, you've taken drugs with them. Let's be honest. You knew them pretty well. So, come on, you helped them even though deep down you knew that they were planning to rape that young woman, isn't that right?"

Billy straightened himself in the chair. "I should have known, probably, yeah, but stealing the lame stuff we took — it seemed like nothing. Big companies that overcharged everyone. And spray-painting idiotic stuff on street signs kind of seemed like art. It's stupid. And the drugs, I don't know about Grady and Roth, but I just wanted to forget what happened to my mom and all that crap." He looked from one of them to another. "But hurting a girl? That's messed up. I couldn't believe they would be that psycho. What kind of a person does stuff like that? And what kind of person has friends like that?"

This time when Billy looked toward his lawyer, he glanced at Mitch, and then his gaze moved to the other three people seated nearby, maybe parents of the other two boys involved. Billy's eyes moved lightly across the room and fell on me.

CHAPTER 25

Jenny

He froze for a second, turned away, and held a hand over his mouth as if he wished he could shove all those words back in. Finally Billy looked directly at me, his face white.

"I could have stopped them." He stared at me darkly, but I wouldn't run even though I knew he wanted me out of there. "But I didn't." Billy turned back to the lawyers. "We were on the bus going to the mall in Evans. There was this girl who was alone and Grady thought she was hot. I didn't like the way he was talking about her, but he's pretty much a jackass about girls. Anyway, he asks me to pretend I lost my dog and to get her to help look for it, and when I ask why he says so we can meet her, like an icebreaker. It seemed stupid, but no stupider than other stuff we'd done.

"So we get off two stops too soon so we can follow her. I came up to her and asked if she's seen a little dog. Grady and Roth pretend they don't know me and we all start looking for this made-up Chihuahua named Taquito. Then Grady and her went down an alley because he said he thought he heard barking and Roth asks me to keep watch at the opening of the alley and I said hell no. And he said then I should just leave, if I was such a wuss. That pissed me off, so I walked away, but a few blocks later I realized that they might actually . . ." Billy sighed. "That they might force her into something, so I came back, but they weren't where I left them. I walked around. Checked in all the stores and food places for about half a mile. When I couldn't find them I thought maybe they'd gotten scared and given up or got caught or something.

"And the next day when I asked them, at first Grady said nothing happened. They acted like *I* ditched *them*. But it was the way they said it. They used the same words as each other, like they got together and decided what to tell me. I knew they did it. And that night I thought how I should've seen what was coming. I thought of all these things I could've done. I could have run around the bus screaming, 'Fire!' I could have got in her face and yelled, 'There's no dog!' I could have just picked a fight with Grady. He has lousy impulse control. I could have got him going and let him whale on me so the girl could have run away. I would've been okay. I have a hard head." He looked my way again. "Why didn't I do that?" Billy words came at me, dangerous as bullets. "Give me a piece of paper: I bet I could think of a hundred things I could've done to stop them. It would've been so easy for me to save her from all that, just by warning her. I'm not gonna make that mistake again." He was winded. He shifted as if having to stay in his chair was torture.

"Son." This was the first time ADA Farmington asked a question. "You're convinced that you could have stopped Mr. Grady and Mr. Roth from raping Miss Dodd. But if you hadn't been with them on the day of the rape, do you think your friends would have raped her anyway?"

"Yeah," said Billy.

"Mr. Blake has no way of knowing that," Ms. Ivers pointed out.

"I was asking him for an opinion, since you insist he knows

these young men so well." Mr. Farmington nodded at Billy. "Why do you think they would've gone ahead without you?"

"Because Grady is the idea man. Roth and I follow along for some stupid reason. Grady needs a helper sometimes, but it all comes from him. He likes wingmen, but if he hadn't had Roth with him, he would've figured out how to do it by himself." Billy leaned forward as if no one had been listening until now. "But the thing is, I *was* there and I could've done something. It was like when my dad beat my mom into a coma."

Ms. Ivers came to attention, not like before. More like she sensed danger. Mitch dropped his head into his hands.

"I could have stopped him," Billy said, as if they didn't believe him. "Maybe I wasn't very big. When I was twelve I was kinda skinny. See, my mistake was that I came at him with my fists and he just" — Billy imitated a crash sound effect — "threw me through a window." He paused, staring at nothing. Finally he leaned back in his seat. "But what I should've done was grab a pan or a bat or something and smack him right in the head. He had a pretty hard head too, so, you know, I don't think it would've brought him down, but at least he would've come for me and laid off of her."

"Then he would've beaten *you* nearly to death," Mr. Sawyer said, "wouldn't he?"

Billy shrugged. "Sure."

"And tell us, why would that have been a better outcome?"

Billy shook his head as if it was a silly question. "Come on. Would the world be better off with her or me in it? Not exactly rocket science."

I didn't look away or make a sound, but something changed. The air was as heavy as a river of mud, but I kept my eyes on his face and forced myself to keep breathing. I didn't know what to do or what I would say to him. All I knew was that I loved him. Even with whatever sadness he carried and even if the boy I half remembered from a dream turned out to be real and walked into the room, I knew I would choose Billy.

The lawyers were conferring with Mr. Farmington. Billy sat looking away from me. But Mitch was frowning at me now. I felt like a spy and quietly slipped into the hall to wait. When they finally came out, Mitch had a hand on Billy's shoulder.

"How did you find me?" Billy asked. He'd never used such an angry tone with me. I was startled into silence. Mitch pulled his brother down the hall.

"Not in front of the lawyers," he told us.

I followed them into the parking lot, where Mitch got into his car and lit a cigarette and Billy stood near the trunk.

"Why did you have to show up and hear that?" he asked me. "You think I want you to know that stuff?" For a moment I thought he might cry, but he was still angry. "Now if you see me somewhere around town you'll think of *that*." He gestured back toward the building.

"Why is someone finding out about the sad things that happened to you such a bad thing?" I asked.

"I don't want to mix up your clean life with my shitty life." He said it as if I was an idiot for not already knowing that. "I'd be the reason you were unhappy."

His reasoning confused me. "I'm sorry about what happened to your mom and dad —"

"I don't want pity," he interrupted.

Whatever I said, it was the wrong thing. "I don't care if you're in trouble with the police — you're a good person."

He leaned against the car, shook his head. "You're saying that because you feel sorry for me — you feel guilty."

"Don't tell me how I feel." My own anger surprised me, but I was right. "I'm sick of people telling me what I think and what I believe."

He folded his arms the way my mother had when she didn't want to talk about ghosts. "Am I the bad boy you can shock your parents with?"

"That's the stupidest thing I ever heard," I told him.

Billy covered his face with his hands like he was trying to figure out how to get through to me. When he looked at me again he asked, "Why would you like me?"

I took a breath and spoke carefully so he wouldn't think I was throwing words around. "Because you defended me in front of your friends even though you got beat up for it," I told him. "And you noticed me when I was sad and you wanted to know what I was thinking when I prayed with my eyes open."

He sighed. "I can't make time go back there. It's too late. I grew up."

"I like the way you turned out. I love you," I said. "I choose you."

He came at me, but I wouldn't flinch. He didn't push me or hit me. For a moment I thought he would kiss me, but instead he said, "I don't choose you."

Mitch started the car when Billy slammed the door. I moved out of the way as they backed up and drove off.

I wanted to fly out of my body, like I used to practice in the shower. But my soul was a stone stuck in my chest, cold and heavy.

I don't know how long I stood in the parking lot. Another car honked at me, so I walked to the corner and took out the phone. My brain couldn't decide which direction to walk to get to the library.

My mother answered with "What's the matter?"

"I'm at Main and Fifth," I told her.

"What?" she asked. "Why?"

All I could think to say was "I'm tired."

My mother had to honk even after she pulled up in front of me. "Are you sick?" she asked. "Why are you all the way over here?"

I got in the car feeling stiff. "I'm sad," I told her, hoping if I said it out loud I might be able to cry and feel human again, but I was dry on the inside.

"About San Diego?" she asked, and her words made no sense. "It's just for a while until I figure out how to deal with your father legally," said my mother. "I want you to tell me everything he says and does — anything that could help us."

I stared out the window, and her words buzzed and hit the glass like flies. All my mind would do was one simple equation — if Billy didn't want me and the boy I thought I'd met and forgotten was something I made up in a dream, then true love wasn't real.

My mother was talking, the car was rolling, I was still breathing. But I was one of those people who's pulled out of the snow and only feels the pain when they're heated back up. If I didn't want a broken heart, I just needed to stay numb. People caught in blizzards felt happy while they froze to death. Drowning people, too, say they feel peaceful when they give in.

I held my breath for a few seconds, to see if there was any pleasure in it. When I started to see flecks of mirror in my vision, I let out the breath in a sigh.

"Are you listening to me?" my mother asked.

"You and Daddy were right," I said.

"What?" My mother may not have liked being teamed with him in that sentence, but she didn't argue the point.

"I'll do whatever you say," I told her. "What should I do?"

My mother seemed so sure of the answer. "Pack, go with him, and don't rock the boat."

That was the opposite of going overboard, I thought. Not rocking the boat. Not making waves.

⌒

My mother had already set out things for me to take to San Diego, piles on the foot of my bed and on my desktop. Two large empty suitcases waited. I heard her in the office on the phone. I stared at the stacks of clothes, the white Bible I'd had since I was eight wrapped in a slip to keep it safe, toiletries in zippered plastic bags. Even desk supplies in a gallon bag. She'd left the bedding and the picture of the praying hands on the wall, but everything else was stacked up and waiting.

I took the larger of the two suitcases out into the hall, empty. I went and got a big black trash bag from the kitchen and shook it open. Back in my room I started with the clothes. I didn't need much. I put two pairs of pants and two shirts, a white sweater, and two plain Sunday school dresses into the bottom of the other suitcase. One nightgown, underwear, and the bag of toiletries.

The rest went into the trash bag. Scarves knitted by my aunt, a snow hat I'd worn in fifth grade, my flannel pajamas with kittens on them, my jewelry box with its worthless treasure, my ballet box, toe shoes and all. My childhood was swallowed whole. Even the contents of my bottom dresser drawer, where a false bottom had kept my pictures and Polaroid camera safe. The black-and-white photographs blurred as they fell away. And all my colors bled together as I tossed the rest of my old life out — red sweater, yellow dress, blue skirt — into the black bag.

CHAPTER 26

Jenny

THE CAINE HOUSE USED TO FASCINATE ME when I was little. Mrs. Caine collected figurines of angels, some of them salt and pepper shakers, some fragile blown glass; some of them were bells or made from sand dollars or walnut shells. They were shelved in deep racks with glass fronts so they were always in the dark. Now as I walked past the cabinet the angels seems like prisoners. I wanted to open the glass fronts and let them fly away.

My mother said the women's group was going to hold a special prayer meeting for me. I guess because my father was picking me up that afternoon to take me to California. I agreed. My plan was to be completely cooperative. I was floating on a river of calm, a leaf on the current. It would be easy to go to church and be home-schooled and use a camera only to take pictures at birthday parties and Christmas. I might learn to be happy. As long as I didn't care what happened to me next.

When girls visited women's group, and I had several times, they sat in the least comfortable chairs, but when we came into the living room Mrs. Caine put me in a large recliner. It was right across from a glass cabinet of brass and wooden angels. They stood in a straight line in the shadows, a tiny army.

It did seem strange that there was no food. Usually they served nut bread or crackers and cheese. There was one small pitcher of water, but not even any glasses. No smell of coffee coming from the kitchen. That should have made me suspicious.

My mom sat on the sofa beside my chair. The quiet was creepy — even more than snacking, these women liked to talk.

"Jenny," said Mrs. Caine. "We have come to realize you need help."

I was used to agreeing with my parents when they said I needed prayers. I nodded. *Of course I needed prayers.*

"And your mother can't deal with this by herself," Mrs. Caine went on. "We love you, dear. That's why we watch over you and notice when things aren't right. For instance, we know that you've been having trouble remembering things lately, like what you did and said just a few days ago."

That wasn't the kind of sin I expected them to point out.

"And no one would disagree that lately you haven't been acting like yourself."

Why couldn't they just pray for me and get it over with?

"You've lashed out in anger at your mother and at all of us. You've been secretive and disobedient." Mrs. Caine paused. "You had sexual intercourse."

I was startled by this. It hurt to come out of my numbness for a moment. My mother had confided in them more than I realized.

"In church, you behaved very strangely," she said. "Almost as if being in the Lord's house made you agitated. You repeatedly threw the Bible onto the floor."

"I did what?" I asked. Then I realized she must have meant

the way I was letting the pages fall open and reading quotes with Helen.

"I know," said Mrs. Caine with an unpleasant tone of pity in her voice. "It wasn't really you, was it?"

I looked down at my hands in my lap because glancing at the women around the room bothered me. They wore their matching sweater sets and modest makeup and reasonable shoes, and yet they held their crosses like they were expecting a vampire attack.

"You were screaming," said Mrs. Caine, "that you were trapped when you were in the nursery changing room. You told your mother that there was a kind of spirit inside you."

I didn't have to look at my mother to feel her embarrassment. Maybe she'd told Mrs. Caine secrets that she didn't expect to hear repeated.

"We're going to help you," said Mrs. Caine. "Let us do that."

A Heavy Prayer Intervention. They'd lay their hands on me and I'd thank them and some of them would cry and we'd have tea and then it would be over.

"There are certain signs," said Mrs. Caine. "You saw someone in the bathroom when you took sleeping pills, someone your mother couldn't see."

I did look at my mother now. Nerves pulled in tight lines around her eyes. She'd told them such strange details. It didn't make any sense. What did thinking I saw someone by the bathtub have to do with dropping a Bible?

"You knew things that you couldn't have known," said Mrs. Caine. "Things about your English teacher."

This must've been from Helen's time. He was her host. Had she talked about him?

"At last week's meeting you knew someone in the room was having an affair," said Mrs. Caine.

Helen was me that night. "What did I say?"

"You don't remember yelling at us?" Mrs. Caine asked. "Your mother tells us that even your handwriting looks different sometimes."

Without a word, my mother put her hand on my arm. Did she wish now she hadn't shared so many stories with Mrs. Caine?

"Cathy, it's natural for you to be protective," said Mrs. Caine. "Your instinct is to come to her aid. But you know in your heart that we're not the enemy. We're here to save Jenny."

My mother took her hand away. "She was baptized in our church," she said. "You were all there. She went through confirmation class and joined the adult congregation."

"She invited it in," said Mrs. Caine.

It? I felt an odd buzzing from one ear to the other.

"We're not just dealing with Jenny anymore."

My skin crawled like a swarm of ants. Why did they have to pull me out of my numbness? The sadness opened in me like a shattering window.

Mrs. Caine stepped closer, standing right in front of my chair. "Jennifer, you have to refuse evil and give yourself back to Christ.

"I do," I said. I knew it was better not to argue. Just agree that you're a sinful wretch and promise never to do it again.

"The Devil tricked you. That's what he does. But you invited him in, didn't you?" asked Mrs. Caine.

The word woke me up, made my ears taut. *Devil.*

"No," I said. My face was burning. I wanted to throw up. "Not the Devil."

"A demon, then," said Mrs. Caine. "But Jesus Christ is stronger than any demon." She stepped closer and nodded to the other women. "Just relax, Jenny. We're going to lay hands on you."

This wasn't foreign to me. It happened every week in my house, but as Mrs. Lowe and Mrs. Baum came over and knelt in front of me, they pressed my wrists down onto the armrests and held my legs against the chair with their bodies. I knew this was not really the laying on of hands in prayer. It was more like holding me down to be tortured.

"Don't!" I tried to pull free, but the women held fast and whispered comforts to me like aunties who want you to stay still while they take out a splinter.

"It's expected that she'll fight," Mrs. Caine said matter-of-factly.

Mrs. Garman and Ellen Woolcott came and each held one of my shoulders to the back of the chair. I wanted to scream and throw them off, but I didn't want to look or sound like a possessed person.

Mrs. Caine lifted the little pitcher of water and dipped her fingers in it, then flicked the liquid in my face. A drop stung my left eye and another hit my lower lip. Salt water?

Mrs. Baum whispered, "It hurts her!"

Ellen Woolcott gasped, let go of my shoulder, and hurried out of the room and down the hall.

"It's fine," said Mrs. Caine. "If she's scared, it's better if she's not in the room."

Finally my mother spoke up. "I don't like this."

"Trust me," said Mrs. Caine.

There was nothing I would've liked more than to run away, but I was sticking to my plans. Go along with everything. Let them think what they wanted. Just be passive and thank them afterward. But as they began to read aloud together, it hurt my feelings that my own mother didn't stop them. They were treating me like a monster and she was letting them.

"Lord have mercy," Mrs. Caine chanted, and the others, even my mother, joined her. "Heavenly Father, hear us. Intercede, O God," they spoke in unison.

I wanted to slap their hands away. But that would be exactly what they'd expect a demon to do. "I'm not evil," I said. But I felt like my body was weak and empty, my spirit was small and cowering—I was shrinking on the inside like a burned-up match. I said, "I don't have a demon in me."

"Don't converse with it," whispered Mrs. Caine.

I remembered the way my father would hold up one finger while I was trying to talk about my feelings or ideas and I would have to be silent. If I spoke again, my mother would hush me. In those moments I was nothing, less talkative than a sparrow.

Be a sparrow, I told myself. *Be silent and fly away. No one will bother you if you disappear.*

CHAPTER 27

Helen

In my personal hell, time had stopped. I was already drowned and now I was seeing the gap in the cellar door through a distorting veil of silty water. I was upright, the crown of my head floating just a few inches below the ceiling, my body hanging below, my hands floating at shoulder height.

This time the scene felt different — it used to scald my skin with cold and chill my bones to aching — now the cold only brought a numbing sensation. I was as stiff as clay. I could see one frozen bolt of lightning hanging in the sky, its brilliance diffused in waves of blue and green.

What tortured me was that this storm would never grow or wither. No sunset was pending, no season change. No one would ever come to find my body.

Better that I should hide here instead of haunt Jenny, I told myself. Yet a hard lump of doubt weighed on my heart — I had abandoned her. That was worse than pushing my baby out into a storm, wasn't it? At least I had told my daughter which way to run. I had left Jenny alone in a sea of dangers, most of which I had stirred up. And I hadn't even said goodbye.

I would have loved to grab the rope of time and reel back in all that had happened. Even if I couldn't go back so far as to save my own life—run upstairs with my baby girl and survive the storm—why couldn't I at least pull time backwards far enough to start over with Jenny? If I could begin again, arrive when she awoke in the bathtub, I could take more care. I would keep my sorrows and fears out of her way. And I would come to her only if she called me. I would never force myself on her again—she would have to invite me back.

Even if time could be moved like tugging a rope, it would certainly be a ponderous rope that stronger spirits than I found immovable. As I watched that single thread of lightning billow through the water above me like the aurora borealis, I imagined the heavy cord of time stretching away from me in the water like the hard, thick rope on a great ship. And I imagined it wavering, softening, then flattening into a ribbon.

If time was as thin and flexible as all that, I should be able to pull it with ease—I could unroll it from its spindle and be back with Jenny. I pictured the last time I had seen her—she'd been sitting on her bed, holding out the back of her hand that I might speak to her. I couldn't hear her voice, but she might have been asking me a question that a *Y* or an *N* would have answered: *Are you with me? Will you help me?*

She was far away, but I could feel her lifting her hand to me now, waiting for me to speak. She needed to know: *Am I crazy or are you real? Am I alone or will you come to me and help me?*

Jenny was calling for me.

And I tried to write the letter that would reassure her. Two simple strokes that made a *Y* on her skin. *Yes*, I am real. *Yes*, I will help you. But my fingers were as still as a statue's, white and lifeless, floating in the dark water.

I wished I could grasp that ribbon dangling in the flood and drag myself closer to her, because I felt as if her hand was tied or chained down. She couldn't reach any farther—I needed to close the distance. And the questions she was asking me, she hung her life on them.

Do you care what happens to me? she was asking.

I could not see her—the water was too dark—but I felt her thoughts. *Yes*, I answered. And a ripple rolled away from my fingers. I had moved.

Are you there? she asked me.

Yes, I answered, and this time I saw my finger move. *Yes*. Two strokes that crossed. *Yes*, I am here. And I could feel the back of her hand. I wasn't under water. I was standing in an unfamiliar living room.

To my horror Jenny was being held in a chair, physically bound by four women. Two held her wrists and legs and two pressed her shoulders to the back of the chair. And there was Cathy herself, sitting beside Jenny's chair, looking uncomfortable but doing nothing to stop them.

"Dear God, spare us." The woman who spoke stood over Jenny, holding a small pitcher in her hands as if it were a holy relic. She was the one who had watched Jenny from across the aisle in church.

"Dear God," the other women repeated. "Spare us." Cathy was the only one who didn't mimic these words.

Jenny held her eyes closed and squeezed the tears back. She trembled and strained with her left hand to raise it to my touch.

I drew my *Y* on the back of her hand. *Yes, I'm back.*

She drew in a sharp breath and relaxed, as tears began to roll down her cheeks. I knelt in front of her chair. On her arm, next to the hands that were holding her down, I wrote *love*.

Jenny shuddered and let out a sigh.

I looked around at the frightened women holding Jenny down, and Cathy, appalled and yet merely watching, and the one woman who wasn't scared glowering at Jenny with something akin to pleasure. I noticed the crosses and the Bibles.

Is this an exorcism? I asked Jenny.

She must have heard me, because she lifted her left index finger and wrote a letter *Y* in the air.

"What's she doing with her finger?" one of the ladies whispered.

I wanted to slap those stupid women, but I remembered my promise to be careful. *There's nothing wrong with you,* I whispered to Jenny. In case she couldn't hear me, I wrote on her arm: *no fear.*

"Deliver us, O mighty God, from all evil," the woman with the pitcher intoned. She dipped her fingertips in the pitcher and lifted them out, dripping with water. She flicked an angry splash into Jenny's chest.

"Deliver us," the ladies chanted, "O mighty God, from all evil."

I drew the shape of a heart on the back on Jenny's hand and felt her relax a bit more, just enough to take in another slow breath. Her spirit was still weighed down, though. Even if she agreed with me that there was nothing to fear in the room, something on the inside of her was holding her captive.

Are you still frightened? I asked her.

She nodded.

"She's agreeing," said one of the women.

Jenny lifted her finger and painted the air with a *Y.* But she was answering my question, not agreeing with the text of the ceremony.

I stood in front of Jenny's chair, right beside the woman with the pitcher of water. I held my hand out to Jenny and said, *Take me to see what frightens you.*

To my surprise, Jenny's chin began to quiver. She still had her eyes closed, but she turned toward me, I knew it. She shook her head no.

"She's saying no," one of the women whispered.

The woman with the pitcher hushed this woman.

When James was afraid to remember what had happened at his death, I had gone with him into the memory and witnessed his most painful moment—I wanted to do the same with Jenny, but she was scared.

Take hold of me, I told her. I leaned down and wrote on her arm: *Show me.*

"Drive out all unclean spirits," the woman beside me chanted.

I ignored her and held out my hand to Jenny. *We'll look together,* I told Jenny.

Still she shook her head.

It's easy, I told her. *Like the flood I showed you. That was my hell.*

I decided to show her my own scars again before demanding to see her wounds.

I reached down and slipped my hand into hers, lifting her mind into my memory. My death scene closed around us, the flood was up to our chins. Jenny's spirit appeared with me in this reimagining of my death. She held my hand tightly and opened her eyes. She turned to me, astonished, shivering. The scene was active again—time had found its legs again.

Look, I whispered. I pointed to the hole in the cellar door, no bigger than a cat, and showed her my daughter's tiny fingers holding the jagged wood and then disappearing. There was a crack of thunder and a flash of lightning. We heard my baby shriek, which made Jenny cover her ears.

It's all right, I told her.

Jenny tilted her head back, trying to keep her face above the surface. She spit out a mouthful of water that sloshed over her chin. Finally the flood overtook us completely. We stared at each other through the dark water.

In that moment, seeing the reflection of my face in Jenny's eyes, a tiny angel in the blackness, seeing Jenny's willingness to stare into the face of a ghost, I was changed. My hell was reimagined. I no longer dwelt on how terrified my baby must have been to leave me in the cellar and escape. Instead I was overwhelmed with pride—my baby had run away from death and saved her own life.

I thought I killed her, I told Jenny, *but look . . .*

I pulled her by the hand up through the cellar roof and higher, to the top of the house's roof, where we sat in the remembered storm and watched what I'd never been able to see before: my little girl making her way to safety. Whether I was imagining it or whether we were somehow able to look back at what really happened, I didn't know. But what a brave girl she was, picking herself up twice when she slipped in the mud, crying to wake the dead but still marching up the road, holding on to fence posts and blowing clumps of weeds, calling for help, not in words, but with all the hoarse cries that her tiny lungs could give. Jenny watched, her teeth chattering, holding my hand for dear life.

My daughter, not even yet two, squeezed through the gap in the gate and climbed the steps of our neighbor's farmhouse on hands and knees. She was far in the distance now, but we both saw the door open, light pouring down onto the wet baby, and a friendly pair of hands lowering to her open arms.

Isn't she a marvel, my girl?

Maybe Jenny had no voice in my memory, but she nodded. Something about her amazed expression made me feel anything was possible. Perhaps I could have seen this part of my daughter's story anytime, but it felt as if the magic came from having Jenny beside me. She made me believe I could do anything.

I threw up my arm and pushed the storm and all its darkness away. Jenny shielded her eyes from the light of heaven. I don't know if she saw the same lakeside celebration that I did, with lanterns in the trees and a smiling moon, or heard the fiddler and the laughter of the dancers, or smelled the crocus scattered in the grass and the pinecone fire nearby. That may have been my personal idea of paradise, but her eyes widened and she gasped in a breath and lifted my hand in hers, pressed it to her heart.

Your turn, I told her. *Take me to your hell.*

I thought she might hesitate, but she pressed her fingers to the back of my hand in a deliberate gesture and we were at once in her memory instead of mine.

❦

Jenny was sitting with her parents in the Prayer Corner, reading from pages torn out of her journal, and she was staring at her mother's shoe, the one extended in the air as Cathy sat cross-legged. I was standing in the center of the circle, looking down at Jenny's head.

The scene appeared to be frozen, perhaps at the most dreaded moment, the way I had stalled myself before my daughter could find safety.

I reached down and on the back of Jenny's hand I wrote a *Y: Yes, I'm with you.*

Jenny blinked and the scene began to move. Cathy's left shoe was gently bouncing as she swung her leg, a nervous habit that I had noticed many times in my days living in Jenny's house.

Dan stood by his chair, holding Jenny's diary. He gripped several pages at once and ripped them out in a savage motion. Holding them under his daughter's chin, he said, "Read." And when she hesitated he said, "Take them and read."

Jenny obeyed, took these ravaged fragments of her writing in her hands and began to read from the first word on the top page. ". . . don't know, but I don't think God did that." I could see that she was humiliated and disgusted by this punishment, but she kept reading. "Not the God I believe in. Could we really worship different Gods?"

Dan matter-of-factly jerked the page from her hands and thrust his finger at the next page down. Jenny read, "I dreamed I was walking down a staircase at school and a guy who looked like the guy from that movie we saw in history class walked right up to me and put his hand under my blouse—" When Jenny paused, her father ordered, "Go on."

Dan took his seat in the tiny circle of chairs, looking smug, but Cathy, arms folded, legs folded, bounced her foot anxiously.

"Read," Dan ordered his daughter. "Or should I have your mother read to you?"

Jenny held herself stiffly. Her mother's shoe stopped in midair. Then everything froze again.

It's your memory, I told her. *Change it. Tear it down.*

Jenny shuddered, but then lifted her gaze to her father and time began again, though I suspected Jenny was creating a new version of her nightmare.

"Why would you do that?" she asked her father. "Why would you threaten your own wife with that kind of humiliation? I was the one who was in trouble."

Dan looked at her blankly as if she were speaking another language.

Jenny turned to Cathy. "And why do you let him do that to you? Would you really have read my dream out loud if he asked you to? Do you want me to think that's how husbands should treat their wives?"

I could feel the loathing flood out of Jenny as she began to cry—her tears made little blue pools on her diary pages, words became watercolor clouds and lakes.

Jenny sucked in a breath and stopped crying. "Daddy, go away." And he disappeared. Then she looked at her mother. "Mommy," she said. "Show me the last time you defied Daddy for me."

Cathy blinked at her slowly, and the Prayer Corner was replaced with a church sanctuary. A coffin and white roses stood at the altar. The organist was playing a quiet hymn. Cathy's hair was longer, and she wore a black dress. Dan sat beside her in his black suit, an arm across the back of the pew behind his wife but not touching her shoulder. Three-year-old Jenny sat in a navy sailor dress, her white shiny shoes swinging. She climbed up to stand beside her mother, straining to see the coffin, but Dan snapped his fingers. The little girl obeyed and ducked down into a squat.

Next she lay down on the bench, staring into the rafters. Dan leaned over Cathy and whispered, "Sit up, young lady." Then to his wife he said, "Teach her some reverence." Cathy nodded, helped Jenny to sit up again, but when the pastor began to give the eulogy and Dan's attention had shifted, Cathy patted her thigh—Jenny lay down on the pew with her head on her mother's lap, and Cathy stroked her golden hair. When the little girl looked up, Cathy winked at her. Mother and daughter floated alone on a life boat of peace that no one could see but the two of them.

Dan glanced over and whispered, "Sit up!" But Cathy said, "Shhh, she's almost asleep." And Dan did hush. He left them to themselves.

"I'm not sleepy," Jenny whispered.

"It's okay," Cathy whispered, more softly, words only for Jenny to hear. "You don't have to sleep if you don't want to. You're a good girl. God loves you. He says you can look at the roof of his house if you feel like it."

"He did?" Jenny whispered.

Cathy nodded and stroked her hair. "He said you can do whatever you want because you're one of his angels."

Jenny tried to whisper quieter still. "I don't have any wings."

Dan cleared his throat, apparently a warning against secrets being shared between his wife and daughter, but Cathy only leaned closer to her child and whispered, "They'll grow."

And at this little Jenny laughed. A sound that crossed over into the grown Jenny, who was back in the chair with four church ladies binding her wrists, legs, and shoulders.

Jenny's face lightened as if she had thrown the roof off the room and flooded it with heaven.

I was again standing over her. On her left arm I wrote: *Safe?*
Jenny nodded and in the air her finger drew a *Y: Yes.*

"She's doing it again," someone whispered. "Look at her hand."
I'm still here, I told her. *I will never leave you.*

But to my surprise she lifted her finger and in the air made an *N: No.*

I was taken aback. *I should go?*

Jenny nodded.

"Who is she talking to?" asked one of the ladies.

"You know who it is," said the woman with the pitcher.

Jenny was releasing me from my promise to stay and protect her, but I had to see for myself that she was strong enough. She'd fought her way through the storm, but I wanted to see that door open and the light of safety pour over her.

Jenny opened her eyes, then blinked at the church ladies and their terrified faces. "I am not possessed."

"That's the demon talking," said Mrs. Caine. "Keep her in the chair."

CHAPTER 28

Helen

Jenny carried a new authority in her voice—when she said, "Let go of me" and tried to lift her arms, the women holding her released her instantly. Mrs. Caine shot her fingers into the little pitcher again and tried to splash Jenny with more holy water but missed and sprayed one of the ladies in the eyes instead. The woman jerked her head to one side with a shriek.

The other women backed away from Jenny's chair as she rubbed feeling back into her wrists. I surveyed the room. Before I had taken only a glance, but now I stared down the women around me with a galvanized intention. I bore into these ladies' thoughts, a kind of eavesdropping more powerful than anything the ears of a mortal could provide.

"Cathy, control your daughter," ordered the woman with the pitcher.

"Excuse me?" said Cathy.

I noticed now a black mist hanging behind the head of the woman with the pitcher, just at her right shoulder. It throbbed and flared when she expressed anger. "If we stop what we've started now, it will be a grave mistake," she said. Her cheeks were blotchy with red. "It'll just get worse." And the darkness behind her inked into such density that I could almost feel it sucking at the light in the room.

I came close to the woman's left shoulder and whispered in her ear. "Heal thyself." She shuddered on the inside, just a little, enough to turn the darkness that was attached to her a lighter color of charcoal gray.

"I thought Pastor Bob would be here," said Cathy. "Why isn't he here?"

When the woman with the shadow hesitated, the others stared at her — she was apparently the one who was supposed to have all the answers.

Jenny stood up and the woman's eyes flashed with fear.

Cathy stood too, holding a protective arm in front of her daughter. "Beverly Caine, I'm going to ask you a direct question and I expect an answer. Did you know Judy Morgan was fornicating with my husband?"

The others gasped.

The dark cloud behind Mrs. Caine disappeared except for one small black flame that came to rest behind her sorry eyes, perhaps in the part of the skull where the ego lived.

"So I guess lying and keeping secrets are not necessarily signs of demonic possession," Jenny pointed out.

"Oh, my Lord," one of the other women whispered.

"Jennifer Ann," another of the ladies scolded, "you're speaking to your elder."

"Eudora Franck," said Cathy, "Be quiet."

I drew closer to Mrs. Franck. She was embarrassed and annoyed and it made her thoughts vulnerable for a second. I saw an image pop up and sent it to Jenny.

Her mother's mother, I called. *In the garden.*

Apparently she heard me. "If I'm possessed because I believe in ghosts," said Jenny, "then we should perform an exorcism on Mrs. Franck, too, because she told my mom that after her grandmother died she saw an apparition of her in the backyard, isn't that right?"

Everyone looked at Mrs. Franck, who seemed mortified. "I did see her," she confessed.

"And if you think a demon's living inside me because I had sex outside of wedlock," said Jenny, "then my father and Judy Morgan must be possessed too."

Cathy sat down in astonishment. I felt a waver in the confidence of another of the women. I glided over to the head of the one wearing the pink striped sweater. Again I told Jenny what she was thinking.

"And Mrs. Lowe, too." Jenny nodded at her. "You slept with your husband before you were married, right?"

"Cathy!" Mrs. Lowe gaped at her. "I told you that in confidence."

"You told me a secret," Cathy agreed, "but not the one about my husband sleeping with your next-door neighbor."

"Jenny, sit yourself down. You are in my house," Mrs. Caine snapped. "Show some respect and do as you're told."

The darkness began to form again behind her shoulder, like a hornet's nest of shadow.

"Sit," Mrs. Caine ordered.

"No," said Jenny. Cathy stared at her daughter as if she had never heard her say the word before. "Why should I? You have no respect for me."

The cloud of negativity behind Mrs. Caine's shoulder fluttered, and I blew it away. As it flew off through the wall, it made one of the little angel figurines in the bookcase below wobble in a little dance of joy.

Jenny looked down at her mother. "Mom, let's go."

"We did not give you permission to leave," said Mrs. Caine.

"And I didn't give you permission to humiliate me," said Jenny.

Cathy did nothing more than vaguely reach for her daughter. Her fingers lightly brushed Jenny's sleeve as the girl walked out.

An argument broke out anew, but no one followed Jenny, not even her mother. I was the only one who watched her march away through the door and down the walkway. She picked up her pace and was soon running. She didn't look back as if she feared being chased — she just *ran*. I worried that she would revel in her new freedom and leap from a curb without looking for traffic, but she made her way smoothly block after block, running not in the direction of home, just away.

I was still nervous for her. Where would she find a safe place to land? But when she was passing a store where a woman was just leaving and they collided, I felt as if something had shifted.

The woman was carrying a large bag of books and file folders. She was dressed in an Indian skirt and had her strangely matted hair pulled back in a bright beaded headband. As Jenny clipped her shoulder, they both stumbled. Jenny caught herself and the woman dropped her bag.

"Sorry!" Jenny helped her pick up two books that had slid nearly to the curb.

"Where are you flying off to so fast?" asked the woman.

"I don't know," said Jenny, handing her the books.

"You don't know?" The woman smiled at her. "Are you lost?"

"No." Jenny thought for a moment. "I'm just running."

"Do I know you?" asked the woman.

"I don't think so," said Jenny.

The woman shrugged. "Well, be safe."

Jenny nodded and turned to go, but the urge to run had subsided, it seemed, because she walked slowly toward the next corner.

I didn't know this woman, but she must have known Jenny after all, because she watched her back for a second and then called, "Hey!"

Jenny turned back.

"Are you my Runaway?"

CHAPTER 29

Jenny

THIS WOMAN WHO HAD ALMOST thrown me to the ground was staring at me, fascinated, but I'm sure I didn't know her. She wore hippie clothes and had a henna flower stenciled on the back of her hand. She wasn't from church, obviously. She'd been walking out of Reflections, a bookstore my parents wouldn't be caught dead in. No way she was one of the teachers from school. For a moment I thought she might be someone's mom — she made me think of a lullaby. But I would definitely have remembered seeing this woman in the school parking lot — she wore dreadlocks under her headband. I couldn't think where in the world we could have met, but she started walking toward me.

"Do you remember me?" she asked.

She smiled at me in such an open way, I stood still and waited for her.

"No?" She planted herself in front of me, her eyes tearing up. "Are you okay now?"

I nodded.

"You found your way home, did you?"

The rasp in her voice and the way she wrinkled her nose when she smiled were familiar.

"Are you sure you're all right?" she asked again.

Like a forgotten dream opening up, I remembered watching her for hours from the top shelf of a bookcase. But that was crazy. "Did you sing to me?" I asked her.

Gayle's arms flew open like wings and caught me up in her rough wool warmth. "My little bird," she said.

Every second of my lost days came back as I clung to her. My first glance of my own soulless body, the cavernous museum rooms and running at the mirrors in ballet class and the view from a hundred-foot tree in the forest and the hiss of waves on the face of a midnight beach.

And finding myself in an empty field with a boy who could fly.

Gayle's hug was a safe place to cry. "I remember," I told her over and over. "I remember."

⌒

She invited me to come in for tea, and I would have loved to sit in the back room of the shop with her and tell her my story, but I had to hurry.

I borrowed Gayle's phone, but that same friend of the family answered.

"Billy's not home," said the man. "He's at the hospital."

My joy was ripped away at the idea that he might be hurt. "What happened?"

"An infection or a fever or something."

I had the terrible feeling that I had remembered too late. "Which hospital?"

"St. Jude's," he said. "Who's this?"

I was afraid this friend of the family would know that Billy had broken up with me, so I just hung up without answering. I returned the phone to Gayle and would've asked for a ride, but she only had a bicycle.

She did look up the address of the hospital and which bus to take. She even gave me enough quarters to get there and drove me to the stop on her handlebars. But when I arrived at the hospital, it didn't look right. There was no emergency room entrance.

I ran to the front desk and said I had come to see Billy Blake. When the receptionist asked if I was a family member I lied. When she made me sign in, my hand was shaking as I wrote *Jenny Blake*. The line above it was scrawled with the words *Mitch and Billy Blake*.

I was pointed in the right direction and kept repeating the room number in my head as if I'd forget it and be lost in a maze of corridors.

But when I got to the right room, the door stood open and Billy was not lying in a bed hooked up to antibiotics—he was standing with Mitch.

Their eyes were red. Mitch had his arm draped around Billy's neck as they listened to the doctor. I moved a step closer and in the bed I saw a woman, sleeping or worse, with two nurses gently removing wires and tubes from her wrists and chest.

Billy had tracked the miraculous awakenings of coma patients across the globe, but it looked like his own mother would not be one of them. I stared at her lovely white hand on the blanket.

I was an outsider—I wanted to sneak away without a word, but Billy glanced over just then and caught sight of me. He looked more curious than angry, so I opened my mouth to speak. One of the nurses blocked the door as she wheeled out a rolling monitor and the other nurse closed the door, leaving me in the hall.

I backed into the corridor wall and leaned there. I wasn't welcome, I knew that. But I had to wait for him. I went to the lobby and sat. I wished I had not sent Helen away—the waiting room was too quiet. I felt caved in, breathing in little reluctant hitches. I wanted someone to hold me up and convince me everything would be all right.

But then I remembered, I used to fly like a bird. And I'd escaped an exorcism—I could do anything. I sat up straight and waited.

Billy and Mitch came down the hall—I stood up and moved toward them with no idea what to say.

Mitch put a hand on Billy's shoulder. "Not a good time," he told me. But Billy came to meet me in the hall beside a little shelf with a courtesy phone.

"Is your mom okay?" I asked. My heart was beating so hard, I felt dizzy.

"No." Billy put his hands in his pockets. "I thought it would kill me if she died," he said, "but I feel sort of relieved. Is that sick?"

"No," I told him. "Not at all." My tongue was dry and my throat was tight. "I'm sorry," I said.

"What are you doing here?" he asked, finally realizing I had invaded his family's privacy.

I opened my mouth but couldn't decide how to start.

"I can't believe you're speaking to me after yesterday," he said.

There was nothing to do but jump right in. "I remember what happened while I was away from my body," I said. "I remember landing in an open field." I swallowed, but my throat was still stiff. "Do you remember that?"

"Do I remember what?" he asked.

"I saw you." I whispered it, as if it was a secret. "You were there." I searched his eyes for recognition. "We played a game to see if we could fly to the same place together. You made the stars move."

"Jennifer?"

A chill came over me like a wave of icy water. My father was standing at the front desk with a single white rose in his hand. He walked calmly up to me and lay a heavy hand on the back of my neck. He handed Billy the flower and said, "I'm sorry for your loss."

Billy took the rose, confused. "Thank you," he muttered. As my father guided me toward the exit, Billy followed.

"Let her go," Mitch told his brother.

"Say goodbye, dear," my father told me.

But when I turned back to Billy, I didn't say goodbye—I said, "Don't you remember? You stopped time."

Billy stood at the sliding glass doors like he was in a trance and watched us get into my father's van. Before I closed my door I pointed to the sky and swept my hand across it. Billy let the rose fall from his hand, and Mitch picked it up.

"Put your seat belt on, please." My father was trying to control his temper. I could tell by the way he clenched his jaw.

"How did you find me?" I asked.

"You're not as clever as you think," he said. "I called Billy's house and a gentleman there told me you had called and where you'd gone."

My father had gotten more information than I had—the idea

that he had heard that Billy's mother was dying and then bought a rose on the way to pick me up should have seemed touching, but it actually felt creepy.

"I would've come home," I told him.

"I got us an earlier flight," he said. "Your mother is finishing packing for you. We'll drop by the house for the bags and so you can make your farewells."

"We're leaving now?" I asked.

"The sooner we get you away from here, the better."

This morning I would have gone quietly. But after remembering what happened to me when I was out of body, everything had changed — it was a whole new world. How could it be flipping over again so soon? Billy's mother died, he didn't remember meeting me in the field, and I was being shipped away like a prisoner.

⌒

My mother was in the driveway, standing beside my suitcase and book bag. She was anxiously pacing in a short path and talking on her cell.

When we pulled in and parked, she hung up and ran to my door. She took me aside as my father put the suitcase in the back of the van and my book bag on the passenger seat. "Are you all right?" she whispered. "Why didn't you wait for me?"

I was about to tell her that I was okay, but she said, "I'm sorry about what happened at the Caines'. But your father doesn't need to know about that." She smoothed my hair and checked my clothes.

"I don't want to go with him," I said.

"Last night you said you'd cooperate." Worry lines darkened her brow. "It's not forever."

Her cell rang and she glanced at the number, silenced the call. My father was leaning on the hood now, his own cell pressed to his ear, smiling like a man in love, cooing to someone and not remembering or caring that we were watching.

"Just for a little while," my mother whispered.

"Okay!" My father pocketed his phone. He was happy. "Time to go."

I faced my mother and wanted her to drag me into the house, call the police, threaten my father, maybe throw something. But she just put her arm around my shoulder.

"You can call me every day," she said.

"Mom?" I put my arms around her neck. I hardly remembered the last time she hugged me. "I love you, Mommy."

She locked both arms around me, shaking. Then she pressed her hand to the back of my neck and squeezed me to her. She gasped in a breath and sobbed it out as if I'd been kidnapped as an infant and this was the first time she'd held me in fifteen years. "My baby," she whispered.

"Call her from the road," said my father, but he was the one with the phone. I knew he wouldn't keep that promise.

As we pulled away, my mother just stood in the driveway, holding herself and weeping. I watched her in the side mirror. But then her head came up. Someone rolled into the drive on a bike. To my amazement, my mother shot out her arm and pointed toward my father's van.

I whipped around and looked out the back window. Billy was chasing after our car on a ten-speed.

"Please sit back," said my father.

My stomach was fluttering. This was like a movie.

"What is that boy doing?" My father sounded disgusted.

As he pulled up to a stoplight, I tried to roll down my window, but my father pushed the dashboard control and rolled it back up. Billy skidded to a stop next to my window. He was out of breath, slapped a hand on the glass, as if knocking to get in.

His voice was muffled, but I heard him perfectly. "What did you remember?"

My father honked the car horn irritably and beat the green light by half a second. We roared down the next block. Billy pedaled after us.

"Idiot," my father muttered.

Yes, for a minute it seemed like a movie, but then we ran a yellow light while Billy was still half a block behind. I turned to see him stop, resting his foot on the curb. He looked after us for a few moments, then turned onto a side street and disappeared.

"It's time to grow up and forget about that boy," said my father.

"Won't there be boys in San Diego?" I asked.

"There will be appropriate young men at church, I'm sure."

"Will you help me choose the right kind of boy to go out with?" I asked my father.

"Eventually."

"And you'll help me choose the right man to marry someday?"

"Someday."

"And someday, when I have an affair with my husband's best friend . . . ?"

I tensed, expecting him to shout at me or maybe even slap me, though it would be the first time. But he forced out a laugh and shook his head. "Judy said you'd be bitter, but I told her no. Jenny's a good girl." He sighed. "I'm starting to think you'd be better off with very limited access to your mother."

"Don't you think it would be better for my walk with Christ if I lived with the parent who did not break the seventh commandment?" I asked.

Of all the things I didn't expect—after thinking for a moment, he said, "I misinterpreted God's message for me when I married your mother. But we all make mistakes and ask for forgiveness."

If he hadn't married my mother, there would be no me.

In a jarring change of subjects he said, "There's a Christian school near our new place, but I'll have to see it before I decide whether to have you homeschooled or not."

"You're going to homeschool me?" It made no sense. He was a workaholic.

"Or Judy."

I'm sure homeschooling me would be the last thing my father's mistress would ever want, but it would make no difference to my father. I suddenly felt sorry for Judy Morgan.

I glanced in the side mirror, but there was no bicycle coming up behind us. I felt myself caving in again, my ribs tightened up so it was hard to breathe. I knew what Helen would do—she'd reach up and tear the roof off of this bad dream.

I squeezed my bag to my chest, and that's when I felt it. The top of the bag was stuffed with things in baggies my mom had tucked in it—a granola bar, some tissues, little bottles of hand sanitizer. But the bottom of the bag felt soft like a pillow. I reached in and pulled out what had been buried—Billy's sweatshirt jacket. I held it to my face and breathed in the scent of him. I leaned forward and pulled the jacket around my waist, tying the sleeves in a knot in the front.

Maybe my silence annoyed my father. "You're my child," he snapped at me. "You don't get to decide where you go to school."

Strange for him to act possessive when a minute ago he had implied that I was a mistake.

We stopped at a red light.

I pushed my hands into the jacket pockets and felt the specks of lint and grit at the bottom. And there were three things Billy had left behind — in the right pocket a gum wrapper and a bus transfer, and in the left an old tardy slip. It was scrawled with the date and time and his first-period class, his name printed BLAKE, W., and on the back, sketched by Billy's hand, not a ghost's, a cartoon of a dinosaur devouring a math book. I smiled and hid the paper in the pocket.

"I decide where you go and what you do," my father told me.

I took a deep breath and sat up straight.

"No," I told him. "I'm the one who decides where I go and what I do."

He glared at me as if I'd used a four-letter word.

"Hear me out," I said, "because I have some very important information for you that you've never heard before."

"Is that so?" He smirked. The light turned green and he drove on, turning right at the next corner. Only one block and we'd be on the freeway on-ramp, only a few miles from the airport.

"I'm not going to San Diego," I said, "and I will never live with you."

"Really?" He was amused.

"If you don't let Mom have full custody of me," I told him, "I'll tell the judge how you treated me, everything, all the details."

His face went chalky. "Plenty of marriages dissolve," he pointed out.

The traffic was backed up—our car sat still.

"I don't mean about leaving us for another woman or lying about it," I told him. "I mean how you held a measuring tape against my thigh to see if my skirt was long enough. How you made me jog in place to see if my breasts jiggled." These things sounded crazy when I said them out loud, but it was all part of his daily routine since I turned twelve. Once, after I'd been to a Bible camp party with a few college-age boys present, he'd threatened to take me to a doctor and have my virginity checked. All I had to say was "And remember how you wanted to take me in to the doctor's—" before me stopped me, a raised hand in my face.

I stopped talking. He lowered his hand. I knew he was furious. Veins stood out on his temple and neck. Could it be he didn't know what to say?

"That's what I'll swear to in court," I added.

"Are you trying to blackmail me?" he asked. "I had no idea you were this far gone." For one moment I thought I'd thrown him so far off his game that he was going to let me go quietly.

"You don't have to worry about me anymore," I told him as I unlocked my seat belt. "Just have your lawyer talk to Mom's lawyer."

Then he snapped. He tried to grab me as I hopped out of the car, then jumped out his own door, slamming it so hard, the whole van rocked. I just stood and watched, with no idea of how crazy he might get. He flung open the back and pulled out my suitcase.

"Get back in this car now or your things go in the gutter," he told me.

This was his best idea? Once he had taken my favorite possessions, the objects that reflected my personality and my passions, and he'd thrown them in the garbage. Did he really not know how little I cared about anything packed in that suitcase?

I smiled, which sent him into a fury. He lifted the bag over his head and slammed in into the asphalt. The clasps popped open and my clothes exploded out. A wind whipped up and blouses, pants, even socks rolled and danced away between and over other people's cars as if I were running away in little pieces, too many and far to chase. My clothes took every direction and fled with glee.

I watched in wonder, instead of the horror he expected, I guess, which made him even more furious. He went red in the face and pulled out my book bag, flinging it right at me. I dodged as it hit a stranger's car in the tire. Someone honked at him. Someone else rolled down a window and yelled. Even if he hadn't been stuck in traffic, I don't think he'd have turned the car around.

⌐⌐

I slipped between idling cars, stepped up onto the sidewalk, and walked downhill along the block where an empty lot stood open to my left, a field with a fence on the far side.

As I stared across the dry grass, I saw something curve out of the alley beyond. A bike hit the chainlink fence and someone jumped off and then tackled the fence like a prisoner of war escaping. By the time his sneakers hit the grass, Billy was running for the cars that waited to get on the freeway. He limped as if the landing hadn't gone right, but he didn't slow down. He galloped like a madman.

I thought I might be hallucinating. Amazed at what I was seeing, I stepped off the pavement and into the field. At first he didn't see me — he headed for the white van, the top of which was visible behind another car.

"Hey!" I called. He stumbled when he caught sight of me. In his face I saw both of them, the boy I'd met in a field in the middle of nowhere and the boy who had broken down my bathroom door to save me.

"Hey!" He pointed at me. He was a hundred feet off and still limping, out of breath, his shirt torn from the teeth of the fence. "You lived in a field."

I'd been moving toward him, but that stopped me. I wanted him to remember meeting me when we were outside our bodies, but now that he did, it took my breath away.

"I remember you," he called, loping toward me. He laughed. "You took us to the Lincoln monument and the Great Wall of China."

He stopped to catch his breath a few yards away. "You took us to the Eiffel Tower." He dropped to one knee, exhausted but smiling. "And you were freaked out when I took us to the moon."

"It was scary," I told him. I couldn't move — I was as light and breathless as if he'd lifted me straight up into the sky.

He got to his feet and walked the rest of the distance. "You." He shook his head. "You took us to a volcano." When he got to me, he took my shoulders and held me at arm's distance. "We had a fight."

I nodded.

"You told me to go away." Then he released me, took a step back, looking astonished. "But you waited for me."

"Of course I did."

He gasped in a breath and came at me. The first kiss knocked us to our knees. "You told me I wasn't dead," he remembered.

"You drew a line down the middle of the field," I laughed.

"I did!" He pulled us into the grass and held me so tight, I could hardly catch my breath. "What a stupid ass!" he laughed. "You took me to Paris and I took you to the bumper cars at Fun Zone! I'm such a loser."

"You took me to a magic waterfall," I reminded him. "You stopped time."

We lay tangled up in each other, leg over leg, fingers in each other's hair. And that's when I realized what the kites had been. Our spirits had flown toward each other when the ghosts had come together in the bodies we'd left behind.

Bless them, I thought. *Bless the souls that flew us together and tangled us up.*

"Oh my God," he sighed, staring into my eyes. "I'm going to jail."

"Why?" For a moment I was frightened, but he laughed.

"That bike back there," he confessed. "I stole it."

"It'll be okay," I told him. "I'm holding on to you. Where you go, I go."

CHAPTER 30

Helen

T IME IS A RIBBON, A DELICATE ORGANDY, so thin that you can see through it to the layer of time below and the layer above. Moments overlapping, lying on top of each other. In this way, past things and things yet-to-be are happening together. The hurt and the healing. The death and the reconciliation in heaven. The childhood and the womanhood. The first glance and the first kiss and the last.

This must be true, for I can see through this moment not only to my recent past and my far past, but into the next moment and the distant future. There was a child, my own little girl. And there will be another child. Not of Helen and James, but a little boy with Jenny's gold hair and Billy's eyes. Someday.

And if time is a ribbon, surely it could be rolled out all together, then looped on its spindle the other way 'round. Then one could unspool it backwards.

Instead of nearly knocking her down, a woman at a shop door catches Jenny and sets her on her feet. Holy water flies back into the pitcher of an angry woman as she stands over a frightened girl. Instead of walking backwards into the dark, I walk forward toward Jenny's window, where I see her waiting for me to speak to her, the back of her hand lifted to the empty air. Messages James and I once wrote fold themselves back up and hide in Billy's pocket. Jenny lies in her backyard as I recite a poem in reverse: *Seep we down as all us of mud make, deep press time of layers* . . .

Jenny sees a forgotten boy beside her in the mirror, but then turns and the recognition fades from her eyes. Then in a bathtub, instead of waking, she falls back into the water and becomes still. I lay naked with James in Billy's rumpled bed and the image of our smiling faces fades off of a small square photograph, which flies back into the camera. In a hidden place between two school buildings, James takes back the sin of his kiss and sets me down on my feet again. After my first glimpse through Jenny's eyes, I close them, shudder, and struggle my way out of her body as she sits beside her mother at a church picnic. I am blown away from Billy's house up into a storm and thrown back to Mr. Brown's window.

All these moments of reverse time are leading to my first moment with James. The fear of being noticed after a hundred years disappears as I look into a pair of autumn-colored eyes.

Look for Laura Whitcomb's companion novel,
A CERTAIN SLANT OF LIGHT

I<small>N THE CLASS OF THE</small> high school English teacher she has been haunting, Helen feels them: for the first time in 130 years, human eyes are looking at her. They belong to a boy, a boy who has not seemed remarkable until now. And Helen—terrified, but intrigued—is drawn to him. The fact that he is in a body and she is not presents this unlikely couple with their first challenge. But as the lovers struggle to find a way to be together, they begin to discover the secrets of their former lives and of the young people they come to possess.

Laura Whitcomb grew up in Pasadena, California, where she lived in a mildly haunted house for twelve years. She is the winner of three Kay Snow Writing Awards and currently lives in Portland, Oregon. Visit her website at www.laurawhitcomb.com.